THE
TENDER HORNS
OF COCKLED
SNAILS

A NOVEL

By M. C. Graveline

PHIKZANA
PRESS
— LLC —

THE TENDER HORNS OF COCKLED SNAILS

PUBLISHED BY PHIKZANA PRESS LLC

82 Wendell Ave Ste 100

Pittsfield, MA 01201

www.phikzanapress.com

Sources & Inspirations

Aurelius, Marcus. *Meditations*. Gregory Hays. Modern Library, 2003.

The Bible. *New Revised Standard Version*. HarperOne, 2007.

Brigley, Zoë. "A Soft Refusal." In *Hand & Skull*. Bloodaxe Books, 2019.

Orwell, George. *1984*. Harvill Secker, 1949.

Seneca. *Letters from a Stoic*. Robin Campbell. Penguin Classics, 1969.

Shakespeare, William. *Romeo and Juliet*. Edited by Barbara A. Mowat and Paul Werstine. Simon & Schuster, 2004.

Shakespeare, William. *Love's Labour's Lost*. Edited by David Bevington. Bantam Classics, 2005.

The springbok logo design is a trademark of Phikzana Press LLC

ISBN: 979-8-9999638-0-2

Library of Congress Control Number: 2025920803

Edited by Lesedi Graveline

Cover design by Giovanna Araujo

First Edition: Printed in the United States of America

For Halle…ke a go rata ka dinako tsotlhe.

TABLE OF CONTENTS

ACKNOWLEDGEMENTS

To **Lesedi Graveline**, whose insight cut through fog and whose editorial gifts brought clarity to the storm. Your patience was not passive; it was a fierce kind of devotion. Your questions sharpened the blade. Your silences gave me space to listen deeper—to myself, to the characters, and to the ghosts beneath the text. This book would not be what it is without you.

To **Marcus Aurelius**, whose *Meditations* gave this book its tonal spine. His stoic reflections taught me to write with both detachment and tenderness, to hold grief and gratitude in the same breath. Each chapter was, in its own way, an attempt to meet his gaze across the centuries. And to **Seneca**, especially his *Letters to Lucilius*, which read like whispers from a wiser friend in the next room. His thoughts on death, exile, and the elusive art of contentment helped shape the moral architecture of these pages.

To **George Orwell**, whose *1984* I have returned to repeatedly across the years—not only for its political acuity, but for the way it threads hunger, memory, language and love into a single, trembling line. His vision reminded me that a single sentence can contain an entire rebellion, or a single heart.

To **William Shakespeare**, whose words about love—tangled, tormented, transcendent—still light the path. His plays taught me that passion and poetry are never far apart, and that the heart, in all its contradictions, is the most enduring stage.

Finally, To **God**, of course, whose presence—sometimes thunder, sometimes whisper—guided these words even when I didn't know I was praying. Scripture lives quietly in the spine of this work. From **Ecclesiastes to Galatians**, the Bible reminded me that there is a time for silence and a time for speaking, a time for weeping and a time for healing, and that love—true love—crosses every border we've ever drawn. If these pages carry any light, it is His.

This book was born of many hands, voices, and shadows. To all who shaped it, knowingly or not—thank you.

AUTHOR'S NOTE

Dear Reader,

What you're about to read is fiction, not fantasy by any means. Its roots run deep into lived soil. This is not a memoir, but a kind of remembering. A story shaped by missteps, by listening, by loving a place and a person.

The narrative does not rush. You'll encounter fragments of the Setswana language, echoes of *Marcus Aurelius*, and letters to a grandmother. These are not embellishments. They are the quiet scaffolding, the bones beneath the story. They carry truths between cultures and between generations.

Botswana is not a backdrop here. It is a presence. A kind of moral gravity. Its patience, its codes of kinship, its unspoken ways, all of it shaped me more than I can say, and this book more than I meant.

Set in the 1980s, in a nation young, landlocked, and luminous, *The Tender Horns of Cockled Snails* follows a Peace Corps volunteer and the woman who challenges the foundation of what he thought he knew.

This is not a tale of rescue or redemption. It is a story of listening, of learning to unlearn, and of love that blooms where it is least expected and most scrutinized.

The narrative doesn't flinch from the tensions that rise when intimacy crosses borders. The characters move through suspicion and silence. These are not symbols. They are souls daring to love beyond what the world finds legible. Such moments aren't dramatized. They're offered gently, because conflict too can be sacred when it teaches.

While fictional, this account draws from lived histories of service, of unmooring, of enduring colonial residue, and of stubborn hope. The characters err, misunderstand, and grow. This is by design.

There are no saviors here. Only seekers.

If Botswana is new to you, I invite you to come in gently. Let the land speak first. Let the questions breathe. Let the characters find their way. Approach not as tourists, but as guests—barefoot, curious, and willing to be changed.

And if you've ever felt the pull between two homes, two selves, or two kinds of love then perhaps this story was already waiting for you.

This is a work of metaphor and quiet rebellion.

Idealism is reshaped by love's insistence.

Thank you for joining me on this journey.

— M.C.G.

"But love, first learnèd in a lady's eyes,
Lives not alone immurèd in the brain,
But, with the motion of all elements,
Courses as swift as thought in every power,
And gives to every power a double power,
Above their functions and their offices.
It adds a precious seeing to the eye;
A lover's eyes will gaze an eagle blind;
A lover's ears will hear the lowest sound,
When the suspicious head of theft is stopped:
Love's feeling is more soft and sensible
Than are the tender horns of cockled snails:
Love's tongue proves dainty Bacchus gross in taste.
For valour, is not love a Hercules,
Still climbing trees in the Hesperides?
Subtle as Sphinx; as sweet and musical
As bright Apollo's lute, strung with his hair;
And when Love speaks, the voice of all the gods
Makes heaven drowsy with the harmony.
Never durst poet touch a pen to write
Until his ink were tempered with Love's sighs."

— *William Shakespeare, Love's Labour's Lost, Act IV,
Scene III   (From which this book takes its title.)*

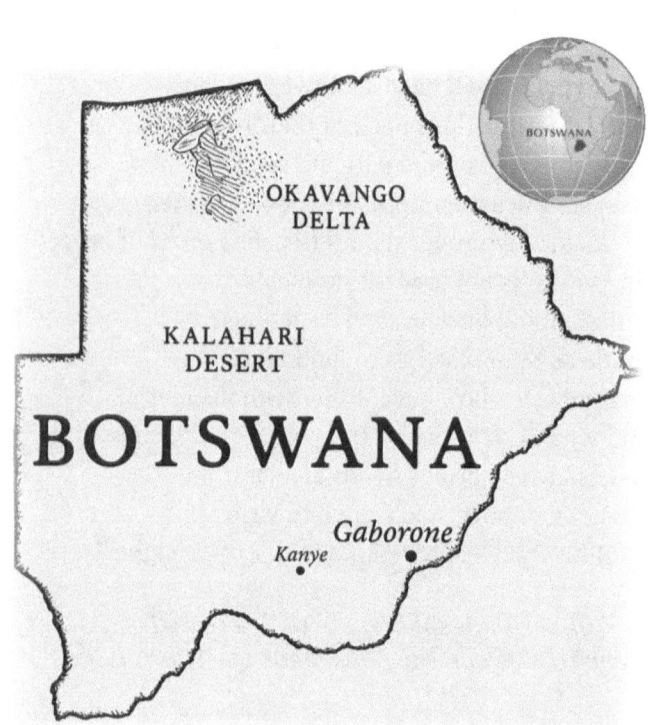

OKAVANGO
DELTA

KALAHARI
DESERT

BOTSWANA

Gaborone

Kanye

PROLOGUE
THE ATLAS AND THE COMPASS

Accept the world's indifference.
Live as a stranger within it.
Bear witness.

Christopher Gardener fancied himself an explorer of
maps—drawn to borders, directions, and the ordered
beauty of gridlines. Numbers made sense. Geography was
order. But meaning, real meaning, had proven slippery. He
had worked his way through academia like a man
ascending stairs in darkness, convinced the next floor held
clarity.

Now, standing with one hand on the edge of an outdated atlas and the other brushing his stubbled chin, he began to feel something unnerving: possibility, yes—but also doubt. Always doubt. What did he actually know about deserts or democracy? What did he truly know about being useful in a place whose history didn't rhyme with his? Would he have enough time to make a difference anywhere—to anyone?

He traced the outline of Botswana again, this time more slowly.

The silence of the library thickened around him. Not a hushed, comforting calm—but the heavy pause of transition.

Of doors opening.

Of the ego surrendering its grip.

Chris thought of *Marcus Aurelius*: *"Very little is needed to make a happy life; it is all within yourself, in your way of thinking."* His grandmother had given him *Meditations* on his eighteenth birthday—a birthday they shared. Two stars born under the same sky, orbiting the same quiet wisdom. That was twelve years ago. Now, at thirty, he still returned to those pages like a prayer. Every year, no matter the distance, they found a way to mark it: a candlelit breakfast, a handwritten card, a phone call that always began with laughter and ended in silence, the kind that says I'm still here.

He carried that "stoic bible" everywhere, its spine softened by time, its margins filled with notes of his becoming. It taught him to hold stillness like a shield, to find strength in surrender. His grandmother, meanwhile, held her own sacred text: a weatherworn King James Bible, its gold edges dulled to memory, its pages perfumed with lavender and pencil lead. Between the verses, she had tucked scraps of her life—grocery lists turned prayers, names of the lost, dates circled in hope. The cover no longer gleamed, but her faith did, steady as breath.

She prayed often—sometimes aloud, sometimes in the hush of the kitchen, her lips moving like wind through wheat while a stew simmered behind her. Every underlined passage was a scar or a song: a sickness endured, a forgiveness granted, a joy too swift for naming.

Their shared birthday was more than coincidence—it was a quiet vow. A rhythm of remembrance. Two lives, two books, two ways of seeking truth—bound by blood, and by the same day each year when they paused to remember what mattered most.

But now, as he imagined sun-bleached villages and the smiles of strangers he hadn't met, Chris wasn't sure what kind of happiness he was after.

The Peace Corps letter had come on a Tuesday, tucked between a utilities bill and a pizza coupon.

You have been accepted to serve in the Republic of Botswana, 1985–1988 as a secondary school maths teacher. That evening, he'd taken the subway downtown and lost himself in dusty books and atlases, trying to locate the place where he believed purpose waited, quiet and uninvited.

He imagined himself a sort of Lawrence—not of Arabia but of African classrooms. A quiet American with a mathematics degree and the ache to matter. But Botswana, unlike his fantasies, did not await transformation. The wrinkled maps and worn pages offered no answers; Botswana, indifferent to his ambitions, offered no flattery—only terrain, only truth.

His idealism felt naive.

Misplaced.

Again, he found himself grappling with self-doubt, the weight of his own expectations pressing hard on the quiet places in him where faith used to live, now tender and unsure. A slow, unsettling shift had begun within him.

This unexpected challenge, this resistance, became its own kind of instruction.

Chris had no idea yet that the stars would come into alignment and a woman would call his name like a bell in the heat of the Kalahari. That the unknown desert he feared would become sacred. That silence could be a holy thing.

He remembered something his grandmother used to say before church:

"If God sends you into the desert, it's not to punish you. It's because there's something you can only hear when the world stops echoing back your own voice."

He closed his eyes and felt the desert's silence pressing in—not metaphorically, but physically. As though it had already begun to surround him. An unease, solemn and strange, mingled with something deeper: curiosity.

White, weightless motes danced in the sunbeams, a silent prayer in the empty space as he stared blankly at African country shapes. He sensed a presence. Unseen, but unmistakable. A whisper of understanding brushed against his awareness: a journey was beginning. One that would not be charted in gridlines or syllabi. And something inside him was ready to stop speaking and finally listen.

So he packed his bags.

He thought of a verse she used to repeat often, sometimes out of nowhere, as if the moment itself had whispered it to her:

"In their hearts humans plan their course, but the Lord establishes their steps."

It had once sounded vague to him. Now, standing on the edge of a life he couldn't predict, it felt like something truer than knowledge. Like something left behind for him to find exactly when he needed it.

He folded his certainty.

And he departed not for the vibrant landscapes of Botswana, but for the profound, enveloping stillness of solitude.

A land unmapped—at least, not on any page he'd ever studied.

But the hush felt strangely familiar.

CHAPTER ONE
THE GOAT THAT PASSED ALGEBRA

Chris Gardener never imagined teaching in a place where goats wandered into classrooms. Yet there he was—chalk in hand, sleeves rolled, patience wearing thin while watching a goat nose its way toward a stack of graded math quizzes, its eyes unreadable, its pace deliberate.

"Not again," he muttered halfway between amusement and surrender.

The classroom, with its cement floor, cinder-block walls, a corrugated steel roof that groaned under Botswana's afternoon sun, echoed with laughter.

Naledi, the sharp-eyed head girl, was already on her feet. With arms crossed and expression composed, she swept the room with a glance that quieted most of the giggles. A slight smile played on her lips.

The goat, unmoved by her authority, selected a page with its tongue and began chewing with a kind of scholarly detachment.

Unfazed by the chaos, Naledi offered only a dry glance and practiced calm. "Sir, that goat has passed more exams than some of the boys in Form 2."

Chris tried not to laugh, but the sound escaped— reluctant, grateful.

Mpho's quiz hung from the goat's mouth. Chris lunged forward, skidded slightly, and rescued half the paper, torn and saliva stained.

"Fine," he sighed, holding up the remnant. "Mpho gets a B-minus. The goat ate the harder problems."

More laughter.

That evening, the sunlight slanted through the windows of his tiny house, warm and gold, revealing suspended threads of light shimmering like sparks from story not yet finished.

Naledi, meaning star, echoed subtly in Chris's mind as he later graded papers. Naledi had exceeded the assignment, again. He made a note to commend her. Not just for the math, but for her clarity of thought, her calm amid chaos, her dry humor. The kind of mind that didn't simply memorize but connected. She'd be his top pick for head girl again next year, no question. He should set aside time for mentoring; this didn't come along often here. He remembered how she'd once stayed behind to help a struggling classmate understand ratios. No praise, no performance. Just patience.

He circled her use of English—more reverently than critically, then leaned back and stretched. His spine protested the long hours of stillness. The room was still. Papers stacked, pen capped, a quiet sense of order returning to the day. It felt, in some small way, like progress.

Later, Chris sat on the step behind his house with a tin cup of lukewarm bush tea and *Meditations* balanced on his knee. He flipped past familiar underlined passages until his eyes caught on one he'd marked in red ink long ago: *"Don't hanker after what you don't have."*

He stared at the line.

Then looked out.

The horizon was veiled in purple where acacia trees held the sky in their patient silhouettes. The world felt old and wise.

What did he have? Chalk, sweat-stained shirts, a mosquito-netted bed. A gut still arguing with goat stew. A notebook thick with half-guessed Setswana verbs. And the memory of a goat who understood, perhaps, that presence was its own kind of knowledge.

He smiled. It was enough. A start.

Earlier that day, amid the laughter and shouts, he had heard Naledi say something quietly, almost as if to herself. At the time he hadn't registered it fully—but now, in the hush of evening, it surfaced again:

"Go ruta motho ke go ruta setshaba."

To teach one person is to teach a nation.

He hadn't written it down. He didn't need to.

That night, by candlelight, Chris wrote to his grandmother:

February 19, 1986

Dear Grandma,

A goat ate my quiz today. Naledi says that's good luck. Maybe she's right. At least it got me laughing, and for a moment I forgot to worry about control. I'm slowly realizing that here, grace shows up precisely when you stop looking for it.

Naledi shared a proverb today, something about teaching one student means teaching an entire nation. It stayed with me. It feels like something you'd underline in your Bible, simple yet deep enough to hold onto.

In the land of determined goats,
Chris

CHAPTER TWO
DUST, SALT, AND FIRELIGHT

Boston. Winter. The sidewalks laced with ice. Chris
standing outside the Peace Corps office, holding his
acceptance letter like it was a one-way ticket to destiny.
Inside: forms, medical checks, psychiatric evaluations. A
dentist who peered into his mouth and asked, "So you're
running away?"

"No," Chris said after a pause. "I'm trying to
arrive."

Two months later: a farewell party. Paper
streamers, tepid lasagna, his mother crying in the kitchen.
His father silent, holding a beer like it was ballast. His ex-
girlfriend, Allison, arrived just before the end, her
presence both comfort and ache.

She leaned in and whispered, "I wish I could go with you."

He wished she had said it when staying was still an option.

But by then, the leaving had already begun, not just from her, but from something deeper he hadn't yet named.

At Logan Airport, he said goodbye like a man might walk into the sea. Hoping he could swim.

As the plane ascended over the Atlantic, Chris pulled *Marcus Aurelius* from his coat pocket. A quote caught his eye: *"The soul becomes dyed with the color of its thoughts."* He underlined it slowly, imagining the sea turning red or gold depending on his own mood.

He thought of his grandmother. How she always left the Bible open on the dining room table. How she believed in both heaven and hell and the challenges we all face from every angle, every day. She used to say:

"God doesn't shout, He whispers. And if you're too busy planning, you'll miss it."

Above the clouds, he wondered whether he'd been too busy for too long conducting lessons in Boston classrooms. If silence might bring him closer to hearing something real. If maybe, for the first time, he wasn't running away—but toward a version of himself someone like his grandmother could recognize.

After a zigzag of layovers and nervous meals, he walked off the plane onto the tarmac at Sir Seretse Khama International Airport finding the air was dry and bright and smelling like something new and ancient all at once.

Botswana's scent is a distinctive blend of earth and wildflowers, the sweet fragrance mingling with the rich aroma of fertile, red soil. In Botswana's capital city of Gaborone, there is always a faint tang of burning trash or smoldering tires. But, as you journey through the country, you'll encounter fresher aromas of the Okavango Delta's lush greenery, the briny vastness of the Makgadikgadi pans, and the comforting smokiness of meals cooked over open wood fires. Every breath felt both old and discovered, as though the land itself welcomed him with its own distinctive perfume.

An old Setswana saying came to mind: *"Moeng goroga ka pula"*—May a visitor arrive with rain. It hadn't rained in days. But Chris felt welcome anyway.

November 1, 1985

Dear Grandma,

The world feels different here. It's like stepping into one of your old photo albums where every image holds a story waiting patiently to be remembered.

Botswana greets you first with its scent—earth, woodsmoke, wildflowers, something longstanding and something eternally new.

I remember you telling me about God not shouting. Maybe that's why Boston felt so loud toward the end.

At night, under skies so thick with stars they seem ready to spill, I find myself listening. Not just to the land or to the voices around me, but inward, toward something quieter, steadier.

I met a man yesterday who told me a local saying, "May a visitor arrive with rain." It hasn't rained yet, but strangely, I feel welcomed, as if the rain is already here inside me, washing away everything heavy I carried from home.

Still, I won't lie. It's daunting. I've left behind everything comfortable, everything certain defined by the kindness of strangers whose words I barely understand. But maybe that's exactly what I needed all along. To learn to trust uncertainty, to recognize my own reflection in places far from where I began.

You always believed we are guided toward where we need to be. Maybe that's true, Grandma. Maybe I'm finally arriving.

From the other side of the world,
Chris

CHAPTER THREE
MOLEPOLOLE BAPTISM

The U. S. Peace Corps had promised an immersive training program, and Chris quickly learned "immersion" meant more than language and lesson plans.

They arrived in Molepolole—the training village by minibus, or "combi," packed tighter than canned fish, bouncing down dirt roads past thorn trees, half-built walls, and the occasional rounded mud hut with thatched roof. The air was parched, the sun was direct, and the smell of goats (and their droppings), mophane trees, and something slightly fermented seemed to coat everything.

Saint Paul's Mission welcomed them with bunk beds, cold showers, and group meals that tested even the most charitable palates. *Phaleche* (maize porridge) and oxtail. *Bogobe* (sorghum porridge) and a veg shockingly called *'rape.'* Rape greens—a leafy vegetable similar to spinach—caused snickers among American volunteers. Rich in nutrients and second only to cabbage in local diets, it was commonly grown and served as a side dish.

Chris invented an internal scale for rating the edibility of local fare. On one end: "peaceful coexistence." On the other: "culinary war crime."

During their second week, half the trainees fell ill. Chris spent one night sweating under a mosquito net, wondering if his organs were attempting a mutiny. Trainers offered salted crackers and the reassurance that "Peace Corps vomiting means you're being purified."

Chris wasn't sure if it was spiritual or microbial.

They attended language classes led by fast-talking Batswana instructors with no patience for English accents. Setswana clicked and flowed, a language of proverbs and rhythm. Chris struggled. The verb conjugations danced just beyond comprehension.

One morning, the instructors taught them: *"Motho ke motho ka batho"*—A person is a person because of other people.

Chris wrote it in his notebook, underlined it, and thought of Boston, of his old neighborhood where people waved but didn't talk. He thought of how often he felt like an island.

In Molepolole, he was learning to be an archipelago—connected, sometimes awkwardly, to others.

By the end of the third week, he was eating the beans and goat meat stew without complaint, greeting strangers with a confident *"Dumela,"* and swearing less often when conjugating verbs. The laughter he received from locals when he tried speaking Setswana felt more like appreciation than mockery.

And so began his baptism by firelight, food poisoning, and the relentless generosity of a place that demanded not transformation, but surrender.

The maize porridge congeals in his stomach. Not with warmth, but with the slow dread of something indigestible. It clings like a misfiled bureaucratic form: heavy with significance yet unreadable. The sun watches—not warmly, but with the fixed scrutiny of an unblinking clerk. Its heat isn't warmth but interrogation— an inescapable demand to account for himself.

Somewhere beyond the haze of dust and judgment, women laugh—not joyfully, but rhythmically, like a coded message tapped out in Morse, pounding pestles into mortars as if trying to awaken a deaf god beneath the earth. He cannot translate their laughter, but it presses on his bones like a verdict.

Christopher Gardener—his own name now sounds like a borrowed coat—walks through a landscape that both accepts and repels him. Each step feels both inevitable and incorrect. He tastes the sweetness of mango but suspects it has been laced with something medicinal. He chews carefully. The fruit collapses on his tongue with an almost theatrical sorrow.

Night arrives, not as relief but as transition into a darker interrogation. The stars are too precise, too numerous—each a tiny eye observing from a greater court. Their murmurings remind him of hearings conducted in languages without alphabets, their logic beyond translation. The word "Botswana" reverberates in his chest—not as a place, but as a decree.

Books flicker into existence around him, half-buried in sand. Their pages are damp—not with water, but with time. Inside, the photographs blur—not from rain, but from forgetting. A ghost emerges, not to haunt, but to help. The face familiar yet unnamable. He turns away.

Baobab trees rise like silent witnesses at a tribunal, their roots curling downward into veins of ancestral silence. He reaches for one, but the bark resists his fingers, as if to say: You are not part of this. Yet his own veins thrum in rhythm with the earth, and he wonders: has he been sentenced here, or summoned?

The Setswana language slides around him— quicksilver vowels, consonants like snapped threads. He cannot grasp them, cannot file them. They vanish before they can be documented. Except one: Dumela. *It lingers. Not because he understands it, but because it refuses to leave. A small, sharp word. Possibly a command. Possibly comfort. Possibly both.*

A figure appears: his grandmother. But she is less a person than a symbol. An affidavit with illegible handwriting. Her face is made of morning fog and lace curtains, and her eyes are filled with the kind of light one sees only after long illness. She smiles, and it unsettles him, because it suggests he has been expected.

The dream tightens. He floats. Not freely. But like a man being processed. Around him, baobab leaves clink like broken glass. Laughter sifts down like bureaucratic ash. And rooms where ancestors once whispered things no one dared write down

Colonial ghosts shuffle by. Thin men in khaki, their medals oxidized, their maps torn. They are not malevolent, merely confused. Stripped of jurisdiction by time's slow erasure. One hands Chris a compass that points inward.

He finds no conclusion, only an arrangement. A geometry of silence, a subtle logic written in dusk. He is not sure if he has arrived, been processed, or simply vanished.

When he wakes, he cannot recall if it was a dream, a trial, or some sort of a homecoming.

December 2, 1985

Dear Grandma,

The red dust here clings like a second skin. It's in my teeth. My hair. The creases of my worn trousers.

Botswana is beautiful, undeniably so. The vastness of the Kalahari, the improbable intensity of the sunsets. But its beauty stands in stark contrast to a homesickness, alive beneath the skin, that hums low and steady.

It's a loneliness unlike anything I've ever known.

Coming here, I imagined a neat arc of self-discovery, a journey with stages and answers. I pictured myself conquering old anxieties, finding a purpose beyond the rigid logic of mathematics. But the reality is less a revelation than a reckoning.

The village is small, hours from the capital of Gaborone. A scattering of mud-brick huts beneath a sky so immense it dwarfs the soul.

My work at the school is rewarding in its small, steady victories: the children's eager faces when a new idea takes root, the quiet satisfaction of planting something that might grow. But teaching is only a fraction of what this place is asking of me.

You always said, "See the world, Christopher. Expand your horizons." And I have, at least, in part. I've seen poverty etched into the landscape, yes, but also resilience, so complete and natural it makes my old worldview feel like scaffolding, hollow, provisional, never meant to last

I've witnessed a way of life inseparable from the land, intertwined with community in a way I never understood growing up. The math I studied feels almost irrelevant here, a foreign currency, like my awkward attempts at Setswana.

I miss you. I miss the quiet evenings, your voice reciting Scripture, the warmth of your kitchen. I'm finding my way here, step by uncertain step—but this path feels longest when you're so far away.

Finding my own voice,
Chris

CHAPTER FOUR
DELTA PARADOX

Lesang Badimo was the first local teacher Chris met at Tlhomo Junior Secondary School in his assigned village of Kanye. The one person there who refused to be categorized. She wasn't warm. She wasn't cold. She was calibrated.

Chris remembered her from his first staff meeting. She was the only one not sweating, not scribbling, not adjusting her cup of tea. Her blouse was a deep blue that swallowed light, her headwrap knotted, a crown that answered to no monarch. When the others looked to the headmaster, she didn't. She already knew the ending of whatever sentence he was starting.

Lesang was striking. A Motswana woman who carried herself with proud stillness, each movement and each silence deliberate. The moment she stepped into any gathering, all eyes snapped to her, caught in the spell of her raw, intoxicating beauty—lips curved in knowing allure, eyes smoldering with secrets she didn't intend to share. She turned heads with her looks, but minds with her mind. And it was the latter that unsettled Chris most.

He had tried to connect the way Peace Corps training advised. Some Setswana. A little self-deprecation. A non-threatening smile of an American whose luggage included a lot of idealism and a little powdered milk.

"Dumelang," he'd offered.

"Dumela," she returned.

"I'm teaching maths."

"That's good."

That was the end of the conversation.

But not the end of her noticing.

From that moment on, every time she entered the staff room, something imperceptible shifted. The air thinned. Voices dropped. Conversations twisted slightly, like plants turning away from too much sun. Even a clock permanently stuck at 3:16 above a dented filing cabinet seemed to take notice.

One morning, midway through the second term, Chris sat at the long staff room table correcting fractions. The scent of cabbage stew from the adjacent outdoor kitchen wafted in.

Then it was her heels. Striking the tile in slow cadence. Click. Pause. Click. Conversations frayed into silence—one teacher trailed off mid-sentence about late deliveries; another stirred his tea without sugar or reason.

She crossed the room with deliberate ease, the scent of something floral—perhaps jasmine—rising faintly in her wake. Behind her, a male teacher muttered something in Setswana. A woman responded with a clipped *"A o bona?"*—Do you see?

Chris caught the exchange in fragments, the kind of Setswana he was just beginning to understand. Enough to register tone, not content. But the laughter that followed was an unmistakable hush, strained, like the wheeze of air between teeth.

Lesang's blouse was cream-colored, almost gold from the window-glare, and her skirt matched the rich plum hue of her headwrap. Not a wrinkle. Not a thread out of place. She placed her handbag on the table with ceremonial grace, then let her gaze sweep the room slowly, soundless, like a shadow stretching just before nightfall. Unhurried, but certain in its reach.

She stopped beside him.

"You look serious," she said.

He looked up slowly. "Just grading."

"And saving the system?"

He tried to laugh, but it came out like a cough.

"Still trying to figure out where I can be useful."

She sat beside him. Not across from him. That would be polite. Beside him—that was strategic.

"Useful," she repeated. "That's the word they all use. I suppose it feels better than saying 'necessary.'"

He blinked. "I didn't say that."

"You didn't have to."

He sat up straighter. "Look, I know I'm new. I know I don't understand everything yet."

"Yet." She smirked. "You're expecting fluency by Easter?"

"I'm saying I'm listening. Observing."

"No, Mr. Gardener," she said, tilting her head slightly, "you're solving. Quietly, maybe, but I see it. You're collecting inefficiencies."

"I just notice where things could work better. Like attendance records. Or textbook distribution. Or—"

"Order," she said, almost kindly. "You want order."

Chris hesitated. "Is that so wrong?"

"No," she said. "It's just not local."

He opened his mouth. Closed it. Tried again. "I know I don't have the answers. But I came here to help. I want to contribute."

She gave him a long look. Not skeptical—worse: amused.

"You want to contribute," she echoed.

"That's noble and a bit funny."

"Why is that funny?"

"Because you're not the first."

He bristled. "I'm not the first what?"

"You already know the answer to that."

She hesitated and then added, "They always want to *contribute* but you think your particular flavor of goodwill is new."

He looked away. "That's unfair."

"It's accurate."

There was a swallow of silence.

"You think because you know maths," she said softly, "you know meaning. But we don't measure things the same way here. Your equations won't help you understand what goes on in my culture."

"I didn't come to impose anything. I'm not trying to—"

"To what? Save us? Enlighten us?" She leaned in. "We were whole before you landed."

He flinched. Not visibly, he hoped.

"I just want to do some good."

Lesang smiled slowly, wickedly. "Ah. The missionary's last words."

She stood.

Chris looked up at her. "Why are you so quick to assume the worst in me?"

"Because the worst is predictable," she said. "And the pattern is old."

She adjusted her headwrap, though it didn't need adjusting. "Let me guess. You read something on the plane. You think Africa is a metaphor. You want to touch something real, raw, and then tell everyone back home how it changed you."

He stood too, heat rising. "That's not fair."

"It's not meant to be. Life's not fair, Mr. Gardener. Especially when you plant seeds without asking who owns the soil."

There was another silence. This one sharper.

"You're a tourist in your own ideals," she said finally. "I'm the one who doesn't play the part you came expecting."

"Don't put words in my mouth."

"Too late. You came here speaking a language that wasn't yours. You'll leave with one you still don't understand."

He looked at her. Really looked. Not just at her beauty, which was undeniable—but at the way she wore it like armor, like warning.

And suddenly, he felt very young.

"Why even talk to me if you think I'm so inevitable?" he asked.

"Because watching is its own kind of wisdom," she said. "Some of us have learned not to interfere with a storm until it's done showing off."

He didn't answer. Couldn't.

She walked away, slow and elegant, like a storm deciding where to strike.

Chris remained standing as the door clicked shut behind her.

He didn't sit. He didn't move. He just stood there, hands on the table, as if still waiting for the floor to settle.

From the far end of the staff room, two teachers leaned toward each other. One of them glanced at Chris, then muttered something in Setswana. Quick, low, tonal. The other responded with a sharp intake of breath and a single statement, clipped and unmistakable:

"O tla bona." —You will see.

The phrase hung in the air longer than it should have.

Chris didn't know what it meant. Not exactly. But the weight of it reached him anyway—like the aftertaste of a warning not yet swallowed.

He folded his papers. His hands were dry but unsteady. In the boundaries of his mind, *Marcus Aurelius* whispered like a distant bell:

"You have power over your mind, not outside events. Realize this, and you will find strength."

But the event wasn't outside anymore. It was in him now beating, rising, raw.

This was a school where every glance carried weight, every tea break was a stage, and every silence had a name.

Lesang had a way of circling—high, quiet, patient, as if the room itself were a landscape she was studying. Chris wouldn't understand it then, but she was already perched at the edge of his peace.

Not to interfere.

But to wait and see where fractures may begin form.

Outside, a chair scraped against concrete. A dog barked once. Somewhere beyond the school wall, a cowbell clanged in an uneven rhythm, tinny and out of time. He turned slowly, as if to leave but paused at the window instead. High above the thorn trees, something dark soaring—distant, slow, silent.

Chris squinted at the sky. He could not tell what type of bird it was.

Whatever it was, it wasn't hunting.

Not yet.

January 23, 1986

Dear Grandma,

Today I felt something change, not around me, but in me. It wasn't loud. No one shouted. Nothing broke. But something cracked.

There's a way someone can look at you and name a truth you didn't ask to learn. It's worse when it's one you halfway suspected already.

I used to think idealism was a strength. That bringing energy and structure to a place was a kind of gift. But now I'm wondering if sometimes what feels like vision is just vanity in nicer clothing.

There's a teacher here—Lesang. Brilliant. Beautiful. Precise. She doesn't say more than she needs to. When she speaks, it's like someone striking a match in a room you didn't realize was dark. And she did that today. Without malice. Without kindness. Just clarity. The kind that stings.

I keep returning to something you once told me: *People aren't waiting to be saved. They're waiting to be seen.* I'm not sure I've been seeing anything clearly. Micah says, *"What does the Lord require of you? To act justly, to love mercy, and to walk humbly."*

Maybe that's the call I missed—buried beneath all the ways I wanted to be useful.

I thought it would feel righteous to be right.

It doesn't.

It just feels lonely.

This place is asking more of me than I expected.

Not effort but introspection.

Silence. Stillness. Humility.

I wanted to leave a mark. But maybe that was never the point.

Humbled,
Chris

CHAPTER FIVE
THE SOUND OF THE BELL BOY

Tlhomo Junior Secondary School (TJSS) had neither clocks in the classrooms nor a bell system. It had Thabo. His promise began at the age of six, as children step into their first classrooms, wide-eyed and curious. Learning, once a luxury, had since independence become a right woven into the fabric of the nation's dreams. Children start their journey in the warmth of their mother tongue, Setswana, before gradually embracing English, the key to a world beyond. For seven years, they built the foundation: reading, counting, discovering their place in the world. Then comes junior secondary school where the path narrows, as it has for Thabo.

Thabo was twelve, maybe. Maybe fifteen. No one knew exactly. He had a dented wristwatch that ran five minutes fast in the morning and ten minutes slow after lunch. His job was to ring the bell—a metal pipe suspended from a tree branch—with an iron rod when lessons started and ended.

Sometimes he rang it. Sometimes he napped behind the row of outhouses and forgot.

Chris learned to gauge the rhythm of the school day not by schedule but by instinct. A rising murmur meant class had started late. An unnatural silence meant students were waiting somewhere, staring at their empty doorways.

"Thabo is dreaming," Lesang said dryly one afternoon as they stood outside the staff room.

Chris sighed. "Of what?"

Lesang smiled. "Of a world where he chases the day's end by the rooster and not the watch on his wrist."

Thabo, lost in his dreams, didn't notice the passing of time. His unusual slumber did not seem worrisome to his fellow students nor the teachers.

The unspoken rule was that time followed its own rhythm, one that Thabo often forgot.

The sun, a molten orb of liquid gold, hung heavy in the Botswana sky—an indifferent eye watching over a land where time slipped like water through trembling fingers. He wandered, lost in a dream without hours, without names. Tuesday, Wednesday. Mere echoes fading into the heat. His watch, a gleaming relic of another world, ticked a silent rhythm no one heard, not even the goats, who swayed in slow communion with the sun's languid song. Here, time unraveled—honeyed ribbon, stretched thin and sticky, folding into itself in endless whispers of "soon," "later," "when the roosters crow." The strict lines of clocks dissolved, replaced by the soft pulse of breath and shadow and earth, a rhythm ancient and unmeasured. Anxiety, that sharp-edged guest, softened and slipped away like a shadow at dusk. Deadlines and ticking seconds melted into a haze, fragile as the fading light. Perhaps time was no more than a dream spun by restless minds, a fragile cage of thought to be shed beneath this endless sky. Where was the goat? Or was it tomorrow already?

Questions floated, weightless as feathers caught in a slow breeze, vanishing into the vast quiet. Just drift, surrender to the vague embrace of now. The sun warmed his skin like a tender song, and the absurdity of it all unfolded like a soft bloom in the heat. End of class, start of class…who knew time whispered like a distant star, faint and fading, its shape melting into the golden haze. Time bent and folded, precious because it was untethered, infinite because it was nothing, an illusion. Shade called like a silent promise, cool and distant beneath the glowing sky. Later? Soon? Never? The words fell away, leaving only the perfect, endless pulse of this breath, this sun, this moment.

Thabo eventually emerged from behind the outhouses, sleep-eyed and unbothered. He rang the pipe once, softly, like an apology.

That day, Chris altered the way he taught. Less reliance on the exactness of minutes. More room for drift, for laughter, for the way learning stumbled before it danced.

Later that night, he thought of a Setswana proverb he'd been taught:

Pelo e ja serati. —The heart eats what it desires.

He didn't know what it meant yet. But he felt it.

February 29, 1986

Dear Grandma,

We have no bells here. We have Thabo. He's twelve years old, I think. Who knows? Not even Thabo. He's our human clock, with a dented wristwatch that runs fast in the morning and slow after lunch. His job is to ring a scrap of metal suspended from a tree branch when classes begin or end. Sometimes he does. Sometimes he forgets and sleeps behind the outhouses. And when that happens, everything pauses. Not with panic, but with a shrug. It's oddly beautiful, even when it's frustrating.

I've been thinking a lot about time. So mechanical in the west and seemingly so spiritual here. There's a rhythm here that doesn't come from bells or buzzers or synchronized clocks. It comes from the goats and the grass, from the sway of mophane trees and the tilt of the sun. Time here isn't kept. It's felt. It isn't measured. It unfolds.

In the West, time is a tyrant. We strap it to our wrists. We measure it in quarter-hours and deadlines, carve our days into obedient rectangles. We speak of "making time," "saving time," "losing time," as though it were a currency, something to invest, to spend wisely, to run out of.

But here? Time is not currency. It is not a cage. It's something else entirely. Something wild and spiritual and hard to pin down. I'm beginning to think that for thousands of years, people here didn't arrive *at* a time. They arrived when the feeling was right. The sun, not a clock, told them when to wake. The sound of donkeys returning from the hills. The moon, like a soft drumbeat in the sky, reminding the cattle to rest. Roosters announcing early morning and day's end with their 'doodle-dees.'

And yes, Grandma, it drives me crazy some days. The lessons that start late. The meetings that happen only if someone remembers. The child who shows up an hour 'late' barefoot and smiling, as if that hour never really existed. It's a cultural rift I feel in my bones. I was raised in a place where time was precise, polished, punctual— arrive early, stay on schedule, respect the clock.

Here, I'm learning to respect the *pause*.

Einstein said time is an illusion—that it bends, stretches, reshapes itself depending on speed and perspective. Someone else claimed the past, present, and future are all happening simultaneously. And maybe that's not just physics. Maybe it's something the people here have always understood that what matters is not the moment as marked by a clock, but the moment as *lived*. Deliberately.

Seneca wrote that we are dying every day, and that the whole future lies in uncertainty, so the only thing that truly belongs to us is the present moment. And here, in this burnt-out place where wristwatches break and schedules wander off like goats, I'm beginning to believe him.

No one rushes here, because nothing worthwhile ever truly hurries. The maize still grows. The rain still comes. The story still gets told.

It's not laziness. It's reverence.

Today, class didn't start on time. Thabo had fallen asleep behind the outhouses again. When he emerged— dream-heavy—he rang the pipe once, soft as a memory, and then ran away. That was the bell. And somehow, that soft clang contained more honesty than all the electronic alarms of home. It said: *Now is good enough.*

That moment changed something in me. I try not to obsess over minutes. I listen instead for whisper of breaths, for the rhythm of feet on dirt in the school grounds, for the silence that says it's time to speak.

Today I reread the line in *Meditations*: *"Waste no more time arguing what a good man should be. Be one."* And I thought, what if being a good one begins with letting go of the fight against time? What if being good starts with being present?

The sky was orange this evening and the children were laughing beneath it, chasing each other through the long shadows.

No one looked at a clock. No one needed to.

From the land of drifting time,
Chris

CHAPTER SIX
IN THE ABSENCE OF POWER

Some days arrive with the weight of an omen. Others drift in like loose threads—just the soft inconvenience of needing to find something for supper.

It was that kind of day.

The school buildings stood still under a blank, bright cobalt-blue sky—whitewashed, windowed, and wired for electricity that had never arrived. Switches clicked. Bulbs stared down like useless eyes. The sockets waited with quiet dignity for a current that had not yet, and might never, come. Somewhere in a government office, a line item had been lost, or a minister's pen had run dry. And so the place stood: wired but with no juice.

There was no refrigerator in Chris's house. Not a broken one. Not a salvaged one. Just a clean rectangle of kitchen wall where the idea of a fridge had once politely declined to exist. Without power, there was no need to pretend.

He remembered something from *Marcus Aurelius:*

> *"You have power over your mind not outside events. Realize this, and you will find strength."*

His mind, for now, was still intact. But if he didn't walk to the butcher before sundown, his dinner would be whatever canned mystery lay behind the cartons of 'ultra-milk.'

So he walked.

The path to the village followed a slow curve, as if unsure of its destination. Barefoot boys played soccer with a ball fashioned from a hundred knotted plastic bags. A woman laughed behind a reed fence. A goat, stood like a bureaucrat atop a termite mound, chewing and staring.

Chris greeted everyone. He had learned that in Botswana, greetings were not transactional. They were sacred. Failing to greet someone was not rudeness. It was erasure.

"Dumela, mma."

"Dumela, Morutabana."

He liked being called *Teacher*. It came with a certain respect, and it suited him more than the mistaken *Moruti*—Pastor, which he still received from time to time.

Teaching was something he had chosen. Ministry, not quite.

The butcher shop stood beneath a rusty sheet of corrugated tin atop a crumbling cinderblock building that leaned like a tired uncle. Out back, a steer hung from a steel tripod by its hind legs, its head tilted inches above the earth. A small boy moved quietly with a knife, carving away at the carcass with the gentle rhythm of someone born into the work.

Inside, the day's offerings were laid bare: flesh, fat, tendon, bone—heaped together on a countertop without ceremony or label. No signs. No names. No neatly wrapped packages. Just meat, raw and unapologetic.

The smell in the butcher shop was both immediate and ancient. Not quite rot. Not yet. But a dense, living scent that sat heavy in the throat. There was the sting of blood, the deep sweetness of exposed fat, and beneath it all, a slow fungal whisper that hinted at time's patient claim. The heat didn't help. By mid-afternoon, the meat had begun its quiet argument with the air. It was not offensive, not even unpleasant—just insistent. Honest. A smell that told you exactly what it was and exactly how long it had been becoming that. Somewhere between life and decay, it hovered in the nose like a fable no one had yet translated.

The butcher himself was not what Chris expected the first time. He was older—thin, angular, almost monkish in posture. His face was creased like folded cloth, his hands stained permanently darker than the rest of him, his apron a study in layered history.

"Dumela, rra," Chris said, removing his hat.

"Dumela, Morutabana," the butcher replied, nodding with quiet dignity.

"Le kae?"—How are you?

"Ke teng. Wena o kae?"—I am fine. And you?

"Ke teng, rra. Ke kopa nama ya five pula."—I'm fine, sir. I'm asking for five pula of meat, Chris said, displaying his five pula note.

The butcher nodded again. No questions. No suggestions. He turned and thrust his hand into the mountain of meat with long fingers, feeling the way a man might select fruit from a tree he planted himself. His hand emerged with a slab of something vaguely anatomical—shoulder, maybe. Or something from the in-between places.

He slapped it on the counter, wrapped it in newspaper with a headline Chris couldn't quite decipher, and handed it over like a verdict. Chris accepted the parcel and gave a slight bow. *"Ke a leboga, rra."* — thank you, sir.

"Go siame." A good-bye from the butcher.

The road back was subdued, wrapped in the slow hush of late afternoon. From a nearby compound, a radio crackled to life, its signal wavering before settling on the familiar cadence of Radio Botswana One— "RB1." A woman's voice followed. Calm. Unhurried. Deliberate. Chris paused. There was something in her Setswana. Not the words themselves, but the way she spoke them—that reached into him like a steadying hand on the shoulder. It reminded him of his grandmother—how her warmth included as much weight as her sermons. And deeper still, it echoed of her reading Scripture in the kitchen while the stew simmered, her voice folding prayer into routine. Both women spoke in ways that made time behave differently. This radio woman, though anonymous, felt kin to all who listened. Her voice was not performance, it was presence. A steady pulse beneath the noise of things. Then came the twang of a folk guitar and the rhythm of a marabi tune drifting into the afternoon air like steam from an unseen pot. Somewhere behind the fence, a baby cried, a rooster protested, and the radio played on—part news, part comfort, part heartbeat of the village.

During training, Chris remembered how volunteers used to complain about the meat. "Too tough." "Smells like rain coming." "Tastes like it remembers being alive." But over time, something shifted. When those volunteers returned to the U.S., they found

American beef pale, watery, hesitant. Botswana beef had conviction. It tasted like the animal had lived and mattered.

Here, cattle were more than meat. They were memory, wealth, and ritual. They were savings accounts and social contracts. The national coat of arms bore a steer's head, not as decoration but declaration.

A cow here could mend a rift—

begin a marriage—

end a life with dignity.

Chris had heard the word *lobola* over lunch one day in the staff room—a bride price, paid in cattle. He nodded along, trying to look unfazed, while privately calculating how many cows his Peace Corps allowance might fetch.

Two cattle, perhaps. If neither had horns.

Back at his house, he unwrapped the meat. A line of blood had bled into the newspaper, staining a hopeful article about rural electrification—a cruel joke, if you had a sense of humor, which Chris wasn't sure he did anymore.

He rinsed his hands in a dented tin basin. The propane stove hissed softly as the match caught. The air filled with the scent of flame and iron and long-delayed appetite.

Outside, the sun descended slowly, without apology. The sky burned gold, then deepened toward violet.

He lit a candle. The walls flickered with shadows.

And he sat down at the desk, selected a fresh page, and began to write.

April 1, 1986

Dear Grandma,

There are days here when everything feels paused—like the land itself is holding its breath. No omens, no emergencies. Only heat and the quiet arithmetic of need: five pula, a walk, and the hope of meat that hasn't spoiled in the sun.

I've been thinking about power, not the kind that runs through wires (we don't have that), but the kind that pulses quietly inside a person.

Marcus Aurelius wrote that we have power over our minds, not events. I suppose I'm still learning what that means. Because sometimes even my own thoughts feel like they belong to hunger or the sound of goats arguing with the wind.

Shopping here isn't really shopping. It's more like an act of surrender. You don't choose what you want, you receive what's given. And yet, strangely, there's dignity in that. The butcher doesn't explain or apologize. He just *knows*. His fingers read the meat the way you used to read my face when I lied about finishing my homework. He wraps a piece in old newspaper and hands it over like scripture.

Sometimes I think the story in the ink is trying to warn me or remind me of something I haven't yet understood.

The cattle here are not just food. They're memory. Currency. Theology. A cow can hold a family together or pay for a future. When people speak of them, there's reverence in their tones, as if to name the animal is to acknowledge all it once carried.

What have I carried, Grandma? What do I bring to a place that has already learned how to endure without me?

I lit a candle tonight. It flickered against the wall. I ate my supper in silence, not out of sadness, but out of respect. For the cow. For the boy with the knife. For the man with blood on his apron and poetry in his eyes.

Proverbs says, *"Be sure you know the condition of your flocks."*

I think that it might be the work of a life—to know what you're tending. Not just animals or land, but thoughts. Fears. What lives inside you, and what you've allowed to starve.

I'm learning. Slowly. Gratefully.

One slab of meat at a time.

With love from the country of candles and cows,
Chris

CHAPTER SEVEN
HARD WATER, HARD LESSONS

Chris Gardener, son of Massachusetts, born to wind-whipped winters and Dunkin' coffee, had never imagined he'd grow sentimental over the sound of water from a faucet. But here in Kanye—a sandy, sun-bruised village stitched into the southern hills of Botswana—that sound had become mythic. Like thunder without rain. Like a promise whispered and then withdrawn.

For more than a week now, nine long days to be precise, the village-supplied water at Tlhomo Junior Secondary School had ceased to flow. The taps coughed.

The standpipe sulked. The sink, when turned, offered a single dusty belch and then nothing. Chris, newly addicted to local bush tea and quietly harboring a mild-to-moderate fear of pit latrines, was learning fast what it meant to haul.

"Village water is still off," Lesang announced as she stepped into the staff room, dropping her book-bag onto the table with a sigh.

Chris looked up from his tea. Lesang—colleague for now. Complication soon enough.

"Yeah, same at my place," he said, trying not to sound too desperate. "Any idea when it's coming back?"

She looked up, amused. "Chris. This is Kanye. Out-out? Could be two weeks. Maybe longer. You'll see."

The fallback plan for such water outages was older than Botswana's independence: the borehole. Kanye had several, strategically placed across its sandy sprawl. Each one was a concrete ring with a steel handle sprouting from it like the arm of a sleeping ox. Pipes plunged deep beneath the village, where rain from another century— perhaps several—waited to be pulled into sunlight.

The water was clean in the technical sense—safe to drink—but it was *hard*. Not hard like "difficult to get," although it was that too, but hard like it had a grudge. Washing clothes in it turned them stiff and raspy, like you'd beaten them with kosher salt. Soap refused to lather, clinging to your skin like a polite guest who didn't know when to leave. And when you rinsed off, you never quite felt clean—just…preserved.

Each school had its own borehole and an elevated storage tank. Tlhomo Junior Secondary was no different: a rust-pocked tower and tank atop that loomed near the school's garden. Most days, Chris could drag his bucket— five gallons, forty-five pounds when full—a couple hundred yards to his little house situated on the periphery of school property. The walk wasn't long, but it was enough to make him philosophical about civilization and every shower he'd ever taken back in Massachusetts.

He quickly adopted a conservationist's rigor. Dishes were done in stages: one small bucket for the soak, one for rinse, and a prayer in between. Baths were reduced to a single gallon bucket's worth of water, heated on his propane gas stove and then used sparingly with cloth swipes. Toilet flushing became a carefully curated ritual, using anything left over from cooking or bathing.

And it was during one such walk from the tank—a full bucket causing him a leftward leaning list, sun high and merciless—that a verse surfaced, uninvited but not unwelcome. A verse his grandmother used to read aloud while folding laundry.

"With joy you will draw water from the wells of salvation."—Isaiah 12:3

Chris didn't feel joyful. He felt like a pack mule with a math degree. But there was something in the absurdity, something almost divine in the struggle itself, the stubborn continuation of it all. The ritual of effort. The humility of a bucket full of water.

Then came the smell.

It was faint at first—metallic, earthy, with a sour note that reminded him of wet sneakers and warm pennies. He blamed the bucket. Then the pipe. Then the rag he used to cover the pail.

But by Friday, his stomach staged a coup.

It started with a low, aquatic gurgle. A deep intestinal monologue in a language he didn't speak but absolutely understood. Within hours, he was sprinting to the closest toilet, outhouse or not, having a sense of urgency usually reserved for house fires and stray goats in the classroom. He sweated like he was being interrogated. He hallucinated in staff meetings. His math lessons became performance art and rudimentary.

He said nothing to anyone.

Chris had a deep and irrational fear of being *that* volunteer—the soft-stomached outsider. He imagined the other teachers whispering: *Look, even the water got to him. Poor lekgowa.* So he soldiered on, drinking tea, pretending the violent rebellion inside his body was just a touch of "adjustment."

But then he noticed: Students abruptly asking to be excused mid-equation. Colleagues looked pale. Even Naledi, the head girl, disappeared on and off throughout the day without explanation.

The staff meeting that Monday was subdued. The headmaster cleared his throat like a man about to announce an eclipse.

"It appears," he said slowly, "there has been a contamination in the water."

Chris sat straighter.

"Our tank—the one near the garden—was found to be… compromised."

He paused. Looked around.

"A baboon."

A pause. Confused murmurs.

"In the tank?"

"Yes. Dead."

There was silence. Then someone in the back let out a strangled gasp. A baboon. In the water tank. For who knew how long.

It had climbed the scaffolding, lifted the hatch (clever creatures), and fallen in. Perhaps for a drink. Perhaps curiosity. But once in, it couldn't get out. And there it had stayed. Drowned. Floating. Steeping. Infusing 5,000 liters of drinking water with the essence of tragedy.

Chris fought the urge to both vomit and weep.

The tank had to be drained. Flushed. Disinfected with chemicals whose names sounded like something out of a sci-fi plague movie. But the process would take weeks. In the meantime, the school's borehole was offline.

Which meant Kanye's next nearest borehole—three miles away. One direction.

Chris began walking it daily, bucket bouncing at his hip like a cruel pendulum, switching hands in protest. Each morning, he set out as the sun rose over the thorny hills, passing goats, barefoot children, and women balancing jugs on their heads with unsettling grace. He tried to mimic their technique. He failed.

Six miles a day, hauling about 50 pounds for half that. His arms began to resemble climbing ropes. His knees composed letters of protest. He dreamed of faucets. Of showers with pressure. Of the sweet whine of a flushing toilet.

And yet, in all this suffering, something quietly bloomed. A strange pride. He was becoming part of the measure of the village—not as a visitor, not as a teacher, but as one who fetched water. One who struggled and adjusted and laughed about it anyway.

Because really, what else do you do when you've bathed in baboon broth?

March 3, 1986

Dear Grandma,

I've been thinking about thirst. Not the kind that sends you to the kitchen for a glass of water, but the kind that slows your steps and tightens your thoughts until even silence feels like a kind of ache.

Water doesn't come easily here. Not always. Not lately. When it does arrive, it arrives as labor. A walk. A weight. A ritual. I carry it in a bucket now—forty-five pounds balanced against bone and habit. And the strange thing is, it's begun to feel like worship. Not the joyful kind. Not yet. But something steadier. Something born of repetition and restraint.

You once told me that hardship has a way of making things honest. And I think you're right. There's nothing abstract about carrying water. Your body tells you exactly what it costs. The sun keeps you accountable. And when it's gone—or worse, when it's been tainted—your gratitude grows a second skin. Even complaints begin to feel impolite.

There's a tank at the school that used to supply us. It failed us in a way I won't describe—just know it involved an animal, and a terrible stillness that no one saw coming.

Since then, I've joined the long procession of buckets and backs and blistered hands. And in some strange way, I've never felt more part of this place.

We don't talk much about suffering here. People just shoulder it. Laugh when they can. Move forward. I'm learning to do the same.

And while I still miss the faucet's simplicity—the way you could turn a knob and summon comfort—I've started to see something sacred in the slow effort of survival.

Scripture tells me that I should be receiving joy from the well of salvation but some days, I forget the joy. However, I always try draw courage to make the best of every day here.

With love from a place where every drop counts,
Chris

CHAPTER EIGHT
A HEART THAT KNOWS MANY SKIES

Two cream-colored combis, borrowed from the district
office, nearly as old as independence, rattled from Kanye
before dawn. Chris sat quietly in the passenger seat,
feeling the morning slip gently over his skin. Behind him,
fifteen students stirred in uncertain excitement. Most had
never left Kanye. Chris remembered how the headmaster
had stared skeptically over folded glasses when he
proposed the field trip—such a Western idea. "A mine?
To look at rocks?" the headmaster asked dryly. It had
taken careful assurances and promises that it would
enhance student ambition before permission was finally
granted.

A second combi trailed behind, with another
fifteen students, along with Shadrack and MmaTshoane.

Somehow, Lesang had quietly claimed the seat beside Chris, her silence as calculated as ever.

"She insisted," Shadrack said with a shrug.

"When she insists, paths clear."

Chris hadn't protested. Deep down, perhaps he'd wanted her there—a voice constantly challenging the ease with which he sometimes slipped into romantic idealism.

Near Moshupa, the combis slowed down to allow cows to cross with regal indifference. A donkey trotted alongside the road, as though entrusted with a message only it understood. Chris glanced back to see Naledi already scribbling quietly, while Mpho stared out at the land, reading signs invisible to everyone else.

By mid-morning, the landscape had turned stark and dry, and suddenly, the guarded gate appeared: Jwaneng Diamond Mine. Inside, enormous trucks crawled over dusty roads. Conveyor belts moved ceaselessly, mechanical veins threading a vast body of industry.

Their young guide greeted them warmly, describing controlled explosions and the meticulous process of extracting diamonds. "Machines see what eyes can't—physics, refraction, vibration. Diamonds reveal themselves clearly under scrutiny."

Lesang murmured quietly, "As all buried things do. Eventually."

The students crossed a catwalk suspended over the pit, gazing down into the spiraling terraces cut deep into the earth. Trucks moved in careful choreography.

"We recover millions of carats each year," explained the guide. "Most are polished overseas, but profits remain here, funding roads, hospitals, education."

Mpho raised a cautious hand. "But how do you ensure the money reaches those who truly need it?"

The guide hesitated. "Botswana has one of Africa's cleanest economies. But cleanliness depends on those in power."

Lesang's voice was low, private enough only Chris heard clearly: "Diamonds aren't just tested by fire. They carry fingerprints too."

Chris said nothing. Her words hung between them, loaded with quiet accusation.

Later, the group ate lunch under a concrete shelter—simple sandwiches, tea steaming gently. Chris stared silently at his food, thinking about *Marcus Aurelius* and his exhortation: *"Dig within; there lies the good."* Yet not all digging unearthed good—some excavations left only emptiness.

"Do you think today changed anything for them?" Lesang asked quietly.

"I hope it opened something."

"They'll go home to rusted zinc and maize-meal that runs out too soon."

Chris added, "They'll remember leaving. Not the pit. Not the polish."

She then looked directly at him and said, "Yes, but mattering isn't the same as transforming."

"Isn't that still something?"

She shrugged gently. "Yes. And no. All that glitters is not gold."

The ride home was subdued, filled with quiet breathing and the hum of tires. Chris watched the mine recede in the evening light, Lesang's whispered caution about echoing faintly in his mind.

***

The next morning, Naledi appeared at the staffroom door, holding a folded letter tightly to her chest. She placed it on Chris's desk, then vanished quickly. He paused, then unfolded the pages. Naledi's bright but uncertain voice rose from the ink:

Dumela Future Naledi,

Today, I write from Kanye, where goats call loudly before sunrise, and the moon watches like an old grandmother who sees everything but keeps silent. I don't know where you are as you read this. Are you in a city with tall buildings, where rain sounds differently than at home? Or are you still here, waking up to roosters and cattle, wondering what you missed?

Yesterday at Jwaneng, something opened inside me. It felt new. Wonderful. But it is also confusing. I saw deep pits and shiny stones worth more than whole villages. Miss Badimo said diamonds carry fingerprints. I wonder what fingerprints I carry, and if anyone will see them clearly enough.

Mpho asked about clean hands. His question stayed with me. When do our hands stop being good? When they dig too deep or hold too tightly? I'm not sure.

I thought of our family. Uncle Seleke died under his mango tree, saying he wanted to rest in soil he knew. Aunt Mosidi went south and never returned, finding a sky too big to leave. Cousin Boi left Kanye, only to run back each holiday, repeating, "Ga gona sepe se se tshwanang le gae." *—There's no place like home.*

Maybe you went away, maybe you stayed. Maybe your heart never settled completely, wanting to chase something you couldn't name. I hope your questions still drive you. But part of me worries you might lose something precious along the way.

I read Matthew 6:21: "Where your treasure is, your heart will also be." *It sounds simple. But it's not. What if the heart moves too quickly, chasing treasure that always shifts just beyond reach?*

Today, I don't have answers. Only more
questions. I'll wait here, holding open this small space
where everything feels possible, and everything still
uncertain. Can you remember how it felt, standing at
Kanye's edge, ribs opening, carrying skies too wide to
hold completely? I hope you still feel it, wherever you are.
With hope and uncertainty,
Naledi

Chris carefully folded the letter, feeling its quiet weight.

Later, he wrote quietly:

March 16, 1986

Dear Grandma,

Yesterday, we took students to Jwaneng, showing them Botswana's hidden bones beneath the surface. The mine felt strange—both beautiful and troubling, a wound humanity keeps open.

Naledi surprised me afterward with a letter she wrote to herself. Reading her words felt strangely like reading my own thoughts. She wondered about leaving and staying, how each choice carries possibility and loss. Her uncertainty was honest, unguarded—and quietly profound.

Her questions made me realize leaving isn't simple. We don't just walk away from places; we carry them inside. Like the treasure hidden in a field, as you once read to me, it's both found and lost at once.

We came home from the mine weary, covered in red earth, but brought back something brighter than diamonds: questions strong enough to guide us home, and uncertain enough to keep us searching.

Maybe treasure lies in both leaving and returning. Perhaps our hearts were always meant to belong to many skies, forever in motion.

Still shining (though uncertainly),
Chris

CHAPTER NINE
HANNIBAL'S ELEPHANTS

The sun rose into Kanye with its usual imperious ease, washing the ridges and scattered kraals in an indifferent, forgiving gold. Chris stood in front of the school fence, arms folded, staring at what could charitably be called "the field."

It was an expanse of stubborn brush, thorn bushes clinging to the dry ground like old arguments, and boulders so large they seemed to have been flung here by a distracted god. Beside him, Naledi examined the same ground with an expression that hovered somewhere between curiosity and polite skepticism.

"So...we play here?" she asked, tucking her pencil behind her ear.

Chris exhaled, running a hand through his hair. "Well, first we build here."

The students gathered in a loose semicircle, some holding battered machetes, others armed with dented rakes, borrowed hoes, and wide-eyed anticipation. A few boys carried the new gloves from the Peace Corps shipment as though they were royal relics.

Mpho stepped forward, smacking a baseball bat into his palm. "Sir," he said solemnly, "we will clear the field faster than you can throw a softball."

Naledi snorted. "Don't promise too much. This looks like somewhere even ghosts avoid."

A ripple of laughter moved through the group. Chris clapped his hands, rallying them. "Alright. We have three weekends. Three. By the end, we will have a field. Not perfect, not a Boston Fenway Park—"

"Fen-what?" called Neo, a wiry boy whose voice always sounded half on the edge of a joke.

"Never mind," Chris laughed. "A field where we can run, catch, and maybe even dream a little. First step: clear the brush."

They set to work. The thorn bushes proved wily opponents, hooking sleeves and scratching forearms. Every swipe of a machete was a negotiation; every pull of roots an argument with the earth itself. The students approached it with a strange blend of seriousness and reckless joy.

Naledi organized them into informal squads: cutters, draggers, stackers. She moved among them like a small general, shouting encouragement and gentle insults in equal measure.

"Mpho! That is not a thorn bush — that is a baby shrub! Even my grandmother could pull that!"

Mpho rolled his eyes but doubled down, hacking at a stubborn root with exaggerated vigor.

Chris found himself alternating between chopping, untangling knots of dead grass, and laughing hard enough to scrub his lungs clean.

At lunch, they sat on a blanket of dry grass, chewing on bread and peanut butter. Naledi handed out old milk cartons filled with water; each sip earned in sweat.

Neo sprawled beside Chris, looking up at the sky. "Mistah G," he said, squinting into the blue. "Do you think the sky is one big softball field? The clouds are bases. The stars... the final score."

Chris chuckled, tossing a pebble at Neo's knee. "Then who pitches?"

"God, of course," Neo replied, without missing a beat. "And the sun is the umpire, always judging."

They all burst into whoops and shouts. Even Chris found himself doubled over, his chest heaving with bright, reckless joy as if a hidden muscle had finally awakened.

When the din subsided, he glanced around at their young faces: sun-glazed foreheads, dust-caked cheeks, eyes bright with something he hadn't known he'd come here to find: a fearless aliveness.

That night, Chris sat alone under his candle's flicker, beside a half-empty mug of bush tea. He thought of *Marcus Aurelius:*

"Do not imagine that if something is hard for you to achieve, it is therefore beyond human capacity. But if something is possible and appropriate for a human being, consider it attainable by yourself too."

He had come to Botswana thinking he would teach some serious algebra. Instead, he found himself learning how to listen to the land, to young laughter, to the unmeasured intervals of effort and rest.

***

By the second weekend, the field looked less like a wasteland and more like a scar healing over. The thorn bushes had mostly surrendered, but the boulders still protruded, defiant and sun-baked.

Chris called the students together. He held up a broken stick, a *"thupa,"* like a conductor's baton.

"Today," he said, his voice full of mischievous gravity, "we learn from history. Hannibal—a great general —once crossed the Alps with elephants. But he had to break rocks to get through. Do you know how he did it?"

Naledi raised a skeptical eyebrow. "Elephants? Rocks? Are we building a field or starting a war?"

Chris grinned. "He built fires on top of the rocks to heat them. Then poured cold vinegar to crack them. We will use water instead of vinegar, unless someone here has barrels of vinegar hidden."

A hush fell over the group, followed by a wild burst of cheers. Neo started chanting, "FIRE! FIRE!"

Naledi reached for a small stick and then smacked him on the head.

That day, they collected brushwood and built small bonfires atop the largest boulders. The flames licked the sky, sending black ribbons of smoke drifting into the bright afternoon.

Mpho squatted beside Chris, eyes wide. "Mistah G, these rocks are like the village elders. They don't move easily. But with enough fire…"

Chris laughed, passing him a cup of water. "Yes, but we must be gentle. We convince them, not conquer them."

When the fires had burned down, the students poured cold water from battered plastic buckets, and the cracks sang out—small, sharp exhalations echoing across the field.

Neo leaped back, hands flailing. "Sir! They scream like angry grandmothers!"

Naledi doubled over, tears streaming down her cheeks, her breath coming in ragged gasps of joy. Even Lesang, hovering near the fence, couldn't keep her mouth from twitching into a reluctant smile.

Lesang eventually stepped forward. She picked up a long stick, poked at a smoldering rock, then turned to Chris.

"You are making warriors," she said, shaking her head softly. "They'll believe they can conquer anything— with fire, and with laughter."

Chris shrugged. "Maybe that's not so bad."

She studied him for a moment, her face softening into something almost tender. Then, with a single nod, she turned back to the fence, where she watched in stillness as they pried apart the newly split stones.

***

On the third weekend, they hauled away fragments of broken boulders in wheelbarrows and old metal buckets. Each trip felt like a pilgrimage. Sweat clung to their shirts like a second skin; their arms trembled under the weight. But the air hummed with pride.

Neo shouted slogans in Setswana with each haul:

"Re a kgona!"—We can do it!

"Re a gata!"—We push on!

The chants echoed across the dry earth, rising like dust columns into the warming sky.

Naledi, meticulous even in her exhaustion, organized the fragments into neat piles for future use as garden borders. She worked with a practiced calm that belied her age.

At lunch, Chris handed out oranges, a rare treat. The students devoured them, juice running down their arms. Neo attempted to juggle his peels, slipping and sprawling into the dirt, triggering another round of wild, helpless squeals.

Chris looked around, feeling a tight warmth in his chest. In that instant, the field wasn't just cleared space; it was proof of something unspoken, a testament to shared resolve and ordinary magic.

As they rested, Mpho leaned against a wheelbarrow and asked, "Mistah G, did you ever think rocks could teach math?"

Chris wiped his brow with his sleeve, chuckling. "Everything teaches math if you listen closely enough. The rocks, the lines in your palms, the way shadows move when the sun is tired."

Mpho squinted thoughtfully at his hands. "Then maybe my fingers know more than I do."

"That's true for all of us," Chris replied softly.

***

On the final Sunday, they drew lines for the bases with chalk mixed with fine sand, creating pale, wobbly borders on the freshly leveled ground.

Naledi measured each base distance twice, then once more for good measure. She pointed out an angle correction with all the gravity of a master architect.

Neo, meanwhile, kept running imaginary home runs, each time collapsing into dust clouds, rolling over in triumph.

As Chris set in place the last base bag, he paused, feeling a tremor in his hands that had nothing to do with fatigue.

Lesang appeared at his side, surprising him.

"They'll remember the fire," she said, her gaze on Neo's sprinting form. "Not the rules, not the numbers. Just the fire—and who lit it."

Chris nodded, his voice caught behind his ribs. "I think I will remember too."

***

That night, in the hush of his small house, Chris sat at his desk, candle trembling against the night's breath. He hesitated, then began to write.

April 20, 1986

Dear Grandma,

Today we finished the softball field. Three weekends of blisters and bonfires, of rocks splitting like old grudges finally confessed. The students named it *Sebaka sa Dinaledi*—The Field of Stars. They said when they play under the moonlight, the bases will glow like constellations, guiding them home. I told them the stars belong to all of us. They said, "Yes, but today, they belong here."

When I first arrived, I thought I would come to teach, to deliver maths like an offering. But these children have shown me that building a field is also building a kind of faith. Each thorn bush we cut, each stone we cracked open, felt less like clearing earth and more like clearing space inside myself — a field within a field. Perhaps every rock was a doubt I carried, and every scrape a soft reminder that love and patience cannot be sketched on any blackboard.

The bases marked out in chalk feel fragile, almost like breath on glass. But maybe that's what makes them sacred: they can disappear with the next rain, and still, they will have existed.

Tonight, my hands are raw, my shoulders ache with the memory of lifting stones, but my spirit feels strangely light. Maybe that is what becoming truly human is: learning to carry weight and yet remain unburdened. I once thought the hardest lessons were in the proofs I struggled to explain as a student. Now I see they live here—in cleared fields, in dust swirling behind a boy running imaginary home runs, in a girl's careful measuring of bases under a punishing sun.

I remember a good verse from Ezekiel 36:26: *"I will give you a new heart and put a new spirit in you; I will remove from you your heart of stone and give you a heart of flesh."*

Maybe that is what this land is doing to me: breaking the stone, so something softer can finally breathe underneath.

From the land of broken rocks and unbroken spirits,
Chris

CHAPTER TEN
ALL THE WORLD NOURISHED

The bell before the first lesson had barely finished echoing when Chris stepped into the narrow alcove beside the staff room—the school's unofficial reprographics sanctum. It housed a single prize: the mimeograph machine, lacquered in the permanent perfume of alcohol ink and slow resentment. It sat like a relic, its drum crusted with cobalt ghosts, each page a reluctant imprint from its fading soul. Even dormant, it exhaled that antiseptic spirit-smell; ink and memory intermingled.

There was no electricity, so no hum of photocopiers, no blinking lights—only the silence of old machines and the hopeful rhythm of the hand-crank. Teachers in the headmaster's good graces might get their quizzes typed on his secretary's Olivetti. Her keystrokes echoed like small acts of authority. But Chris, still new and awkward in the school's invisible economy of favor, wrote his tests by hand. Slow, deliberate. Cursive softened by candlelight at his home, the paper creased from leaning on books instead of desks.

He reached to toss a torn stencil into the wastebasket. And then paused.

There it was.

A single sheet of foolscap curled at the corners, blue ink still ghosting faintly across the paper, the scent unmistakable. He lifted it gently, already knowing. The phrasing on Problem Two, the cross-out and careful rewrite beside Question Four, the slanted loop of his lowercase "f"—it was his. A test he'd written for Form 1.

But this copy bore a new heading: Form 2.

Someone had taken it. Run it through the machine. Distributed it. Used it.

He stared down at it for a long while, a wave rising in his throat. Not anger. Not yet. But that old, hollow ache that came from being seen only after the fact. There was no signature. No request. Only his handwriting, stripped of context and scattered into other hands.

Something pulled taut within him. It felt like someone had dug into his quiet hours, carried away something raw and unpolished. This wasn't just about a test. It was about paper turned ghost. Hours gone without witness. The illusion that labor earned ownership—or even just a little recognition.

He entered the staff room with the test trembling in his hand like a verdict. The air inside was steeped with bush tea steam and the smell of overcooked cabbage. Heat hung stalled midair, forming a low ceiling thick with sweat and silence. MmaSebego sat by the bookshelves, her head bowed in judgment over a stack of compositions, eyes refusing to lift.

"Who used *my* math test?"

The question arrived like a thrown stone.

The ripple spread.

Pens stopped.

Teacups stilled.

No answer.

"I'm serious. This test—" he held it up like sacred text, "—was mine. I gave it to Form 1. Now it's everywhere..."

MmaSebego's voice rose like a puff of steam. "It was a good test."

Chris blinked. "That's not the point."

"No?" she asked softly. "Then what is?"

"It's about respect," he said. "The time I put into shaping something that fit them."

"You were away Monday," she said. "I needed a test. Yours was in the stack."

"In the stack?" He gave a short laugh. "Like something left out for anyone to take?"

She looked up at last. Very patient. Not defensive. Level, like a scale already tipped.

"Around here, we borrow what we need. A spoon. A chair. A test."

"So nothing belongs to anyone? Not even what we create?"

"It does," she said. Calm. "Only yours believed it had an owner."

Shadrack stirred his tea. "This is not America, Chris."

Chris turned toward him, voice raw. "So authorship evaporates at the equator?"

Again, silence—thicker now. The kind that presses hard against the ribs.

Then she entered.

Lesang.

She crossed the threshold as if stepping neatly into a waiting parable. Skirt hem spotted with red earth, a folder pressed beneath one arm like a sealed confession. She stopped precisely at the edge of their tension.

"What's happened now?" she asked, her voice even, faintly amused.

"MmaSebego used my test without asking."

"Ah," she said, drawing it out like a thread being pulled. "A sacred manuscript then?"

Chris bristled. "You think this is funny?"

She walked toward him, calm as drought. Took the test from his hand—not abruptly, but with an eerie inevitability. She glanced at it, returned it, fingers brushing his like a whisper.

"You want it back?" she asked. "To tuck it safely under your pillow?"

"I want it acknowledged."

"You confuse authorship with ownership," she said. "With power."

He stared. "You always do this."

"Do what?"

"Circle. Undermine. Wait for someone to bleed, then say the wound was always there."

Her eyes narrowed, almost imperceptibly. But enough.

"You mistake your work for your worth," she said. "That's dangerous and how people break—quietly, and convinced they were right."

"You're dangerous."

She tilted her head. "You came here thinking effort earns immunity. It doesn't."

"Why are you even in this conversation?"

"Because you've made it loud enough to require witnesses from the entire staff."

"Okay then, let's go," he said. "Outside."

"As you wish."

They passed beyond the veranda, toward the fence where thornbush and wire sagged like tired elders. The sun was high, casting spears of heat that bent even the shadows.

Chris stopped. "I am weary—not from work, but from being foreign. Always observed. Always slightly incorrect."

"Good," she said. "Then you've started telling the truth."

"I write these things at night," he said, "trying to shape something that respects them. And then it's everywhere. Diluted. Like I'm just a tap someone turned on."

"You are," she said. "A vessel. You pour. That's it."

"I just wanted to teach with integrity."

"No. You wanted to be seen teaching with integrity."

He flinched. "You don't know me."

"I know the type. Good intentions wrapped in glass. Always surprised when the wind breaks something."

He stepped back, ashamed of his own height, his voice, his foreignness. And she—always there, perched on the fringes.

"Why do you always come when I'm at my worst?" he asked.

"Because I know when the bones will be exposed."

She said it not with malice, only certainty. As if the words had been lying in wait.

Then she was gone.

He lingered. The quiet was safer than reentry. A thorn had worked its way into the cuff of his trousers. He didn't remove it.

He watched her figure vanish between the acacia posts making her way back to the staff room and thought of the line from Love's Labour's Lost: *They are the books, the arts, the academes, that show, contain and nourish all the world.* How little he understood the world he'd come to nourish. How thin his pages felt beside theirs.

It struck him then—not all wisdom wears robes or speaks in classrooms. Some walk barefoot with dirt at their hems, offering rebuke in the cadence of inevitability. Lesang, like a prophecy, had appeared only when his guard was down—his ego bloated, his hunger for admiration laid bare.

She did not wound him but merely revealed the wound already present.

Even prophets carry no balm—only the mirror.

He crossed the yard slowly. Chickens darted past. The world resumed its turning.

Something in him had begun to be undone.

He'd thought himself principled.

Each step now sounded like hollow pride.

Was it the test he defended—or the scaffolding of his own importance?

Chris remembered the evening years ago when he solved his first original proof, alone beneath the yellow lamp in a deserted university library. The final line had appeared on the page like revelation, the logic elegant and irrefutable, as satisfying as the click of a well-made lock. He had signed his name beneath it, pressed deep with pride, certain the world would recognize its worth. But when he presented it to his professor, the older man barely glanced up, stuttering only, "Proofs belong to mathematics, Chris—not mathematicians."

Now, standing in Botswana's heat, he felt again that flush of disappointment, ego gently bruised. Perhaps wisdom wasn't pride in discovery but accepting that truth was never his alone. Lesang's words returned quietly: *You mistake your work for your worth.*

Marcus Aurelius: *"It is not what others do, but your own actions that should concern you."*

He passed the outdoor kitchen. Smoke rose like a tired benediction.

Maybe the test had been borrowed. But not wasted. By the time he reached his classroom, he no longer felt stolen from.

Just stripped.

And perhaps freer for it.

April 10, 1986

Dear Grandma,

I lost my temper today. I wish I could say it was righteous—but truthfully, it was pride. Another teacher used my test without asking. I stormed into the staff room waving it like scripture, demanding credit. And then Lesang—yes, her—cut me down with a few quiet words. I hated her for being right. Hated myself more for making it so easy.

After she left, I stood there holding the paper.

Then I burned it.

Not in fury. In acknowledgment.

Maybe what I made wasn't mine to keep—just mine to pass along.

Proverbs says: *"Let another praise you, and not your own mouth."*

I'm learning that good intentions, too, have sharp edges.
And maybe love—for students, for learning, for this
place means choosing usefulness over recognition.

With a hopeful heart,
Chris

P.S. Before bed I found myself whispering something—
not quite a prayer, but close:

> *Let not my labor bind me to pride,*
> *Nor ashes blind me to what fire gave.*
> *If meaning scatters, let none be denied,*
> *What wind may carry, or what silence save.*

CHAPTER ELEVEN
SHEBEEN NIGHTS

Kanye shimmered beneath a moon like bleached bone.
The village was stitched into the southern ridges of
Botswana, where customs were not just kept but lived.
Seasons dictated the tempo. During the rains, donkeys
carved furrows into the red earth, and prayers rose with
the clouds. In the dry season, sweat salted the harvest, and
the kgotla filled with stories, grievances, and the hum of
ancestral law.

Tonight, the kgotla was quiet. But the shebeen
throbbed. Each village has at least one shebeen, essentially
an illegal bar, a speakeasy, though most are anything but
hidden. Larger villages have more, strategically sprouted
to serve alcohol to an eager dehydrated audience.

This particular shebeen leaned like a man unsure of his convictions—cinder-block walls, a corrugated tin roof, and the faint outline of a mural from some distant era: a giraffe with the eyes of a prophet, its neck arching toward peeling skies. It had prison-bar doors to guard its cargo, though inside, any notion of justice was drowned in buckets of sorghum beer and cheap whiskey. The place reeked of old bread, oil-slick skin, and history that refused to dry out.

Chris hesitated at the entrance. He wasn't supposed to be here. He'd been told as much by colleagues and by students. This was no classroom where students automatically respected his presence as an authority figure, a teacher. No, this place reminded him of drinking establishments in the seedier parts of Boston…the 'Combat Zone.'

But he came anyway thinking immersion into the Setswana culture would do him good.

"Hey, lekgowa! Mpha madi, ke batla go reka biri!" Someone shouted across the haze —Hey white man, give me money, I want to buy some beer!

Laughter like bottle glass tumbling down a staircase. Not cruel exactly but serrated with something untranslatable.

He smiled, awkwardly. Bowed his head slightly. *"Ga ke na madi. Ke moithaopi."* —I have no money. I am a volunteer.

A second roar of laughter. Was it his accent? Or the absurdity of believing his claim to have no money while arriving at a bar?

Lekgowa. The word clung like Kalahari dust— fine, constant, inescapable.

It meant white man, yes—but that was only the outer shell. Inside, it echoed with layers. *Foreigner. One who doesn't belong. One who arrives with coins and clean shoes.* It had been shouted at missionaries, whispered in awe, muttered in resentment. In older tongues, it was said to mean *the thing that was spit out from the sea,* and perhaps it did. David Livingstone had passed through Botswana with his gospel and his gaze, wrapped in good intentions and imperial maps. He, too, had been a *lekgowa*—bringing Christ, quinine, and the whisper of British Parliament.

Over time, the word grew fat with meaning. In remote schoolyards and kraals, even a Motswana with money—land, cars, a certain way of presenting himself— might be called *lekgowa*. Not because of anything to do with his skin color, but because of the invisible currency he carried. *Lekgowa* could mean power cloaked in unfamiliarity. The rich, the foreign, the unreachable.

Chris felt all of it pressing against him now. A home-grown beer in his hand—lukewarm and sour as regret—made him gag. It tasted like the yeast had gotten into a fistfight with the past and lost. He coughed onto his sleeve. Someone smirked.

So he forked over the pula for a cold canned beer. The good stuff—retrieved from the propane-powered fridge behind the counter. The proprietor, a woman with a lazy eye and a scar that told its own novel, unlocked the fridge like a priest unveiling a reliquary. The cold hiss of the can in his hand felt almost holy.

He stepped aside, nursing the drink, letting the night take his edges.

Then she appeared.

He had never seen her before.

Something in her expression said she had already read him. Not just his name or his profession or his polite Setswana phrases—but something deeper. The secret worry beneath his teacher's calm. The loneliness he hadn't yet named. The way he winced when someone called him *lekgowa*, not because it was wrong, but because it was right in ways he could not yet defend.

She stopped. Close enough for him to smell eucalyptus and firewood in her skin.

"You're the teacher," she said, voice low, musical.

Chris opened his mouth, then closed it. He was suddenly aware of everything, his posture, the sweat at his collar, the past clinking in his pocket like coins.

He caught his breath. Not merely at her beauty, which struck like sunlight through stained glass, but because her gaze held the uncanny stillness of someone who had already read the chapters of him he hadn't written yet.

"Do you dance, white man?" she asked, her voice soft but firm, eyes twinkling with gentle mischief.

"Go le gonnye" —a little, Chris said too quickly.

She laughed, her smile lighting the dim room.

"My name is Heaven," she said, extending her hand confidently.

"Leina la me ke, Chris," he replied, trying to steady his voice in his best Setswana to formally tell her his name.

Heaven raised an eyebrow, "Are you trying to impress me by bringing my mother tongue into this introduction? I can guarantee you that my English is better than your Setswana."

"Ga ke itse," —I don't know, Chris blurted out stupidly.

"Well, Chris, let's see what your feet have to say."

Ten minutes later, he was awkwardly shifting in rhythm while the shebeen swayed with blaring, distorted music and foot stomps of its inebriated patrons. Heaven moved effortlessly beside him, guiding him without words.

She touched him at some point during their shuffling. The graze against his arm was light, her laugh easy, and Chris felt something stir within him. An unfamiliar sense of belonging he hadn't expected.

She moved like someone who had always known the room would bend around her. Heaven Mabono had the presence of someone shaped by more than years. Born before the flag flew, she came from a time when cattle paths measured the day, and tradition sat at every fire. Her village lay tucked among dry fields and whispering hills, where kinship was both compass and inheritance.

Heaven was raised in a cluster of thatched huts, dust-ringed and half-shadowed by thorn trees. Mornings began with water fetched on foot and fire coaxed from last night's embers. Her world turned with the seasons—planting, harvest, mourning, praise. She tended siblings, scattered maize, gathered wood. She listened before speaking, watched before acting. Education came as far as it could, then life took the reins. No degree hung on a wall, but her mind held its own architecture. Quiet, resilient, unsentimental.

She dressed with care, not for attention but for self-respect. Her laughter came easily, but never freely.

She carried herself with a kind of magnetic paradox: grounded yet electric, warm but edged, capable of pulling you in while daring you to misunderstand her.

He returned home late, ears ringing. Keith Richards of The Rolling Stones once said, 'distortion can be fun,' but the shebeen had only two settings—off and ear-splitting. The term *lekgowa* still clung, but so did the memory of Heaven's smile.

She was unforgettable because of the charge she left behind. Her eyes sparked with mischief, her voice carried its own cadence, and her humor disarmed like a story you didn't know you needed. She left people not dazzled but *changed*, a little more alive than before.

Later, Chris remembered what *lekgowa* once meant— "a thing spit from the sea." Uninvited. Colonial. Strange.

That night, by candlelight, he opened *Meditations* again.:

"Waste no more time arguing what a good man should be. Be one."

The philosopher's command echoed louder than the shebeen's drums. He thought of *lekgowa* again—less as a slur than a summons. Maybe he couldn't change the word. But he could choose how he stood inside it.

Heaven.

The candle flickered, its light uncertain but insistent.

What would it mean to *be one*?

The question hung in the stillness, patient and unblinking.

He wrote:

April 22, 1986

Dear Grandma,

Happy Birthday! I thought of you, as I always do on this day we share. And I thought of that copy of *Meditations* you gave me. It's here with me, dog-eared and dust-streaked, in a place where time moves differently and the donkeys seem to know everything.

Tonight, something unexpected happened. I met a woman named Heaven.

It was at a *shebeen*, one of those unsanctioned village bars made of concrete, tin, and secrets. You wouldn't believe the place, Grandma—tilted walls, a giraffe painted on the outside like it was watching the whole village grow old. The music was loud enough to rattle your bones, and the air smelled of sweat, spilled sorghum beer, and stories too fermented to retell.

I wasn't supposed to be there. Everyone said so. Even my own better judgment. But I went. Maybe I needed to know what existed outside the classroom. Maybe I wanted to see if the line between belonging and exile could be walked with rhythm.

The first words I ever remember hearing here, in those uncertain early days, were: *Mpha madi, lekgowa!*—Give me money, white man! I heard it everywhere. In the streets, the markets, even from children whose eyes were too young to carry that kind of inheritance. It clung to me, that word—*lekgowa*. At first, I thought it simply meant "white." But like everything here, it's layered and complicated by history.

Lekgowa is skin, yes. But it's also distance. It's wealth. It's the thing that came from the sea—or was spit out by it. When Livingstone walked through this region with his Bibles and his compass that always pointed home, he was a *lekgowa*. And somehow, even now, I walk in that wake.

Tonight shouted it at me again…but then came Heaven.

She moved like she belonged in every room she entered, like time bowed its head slightly as she passed. She spoke English with the ease of someone who'd grown up reading it in government books but had never let it replace the fire of her mother tongue.

When she asked if I danced, like an idiot, I said, 'I don't know.' Minutes later, I was stumbling across the concrete floor while she laughed—not at me, but around me, like laughter was a language only she had mastered and was kind enough to share.

She touched my arm at one point—lightly, barely a brush—and something settled in me. A silence I didn't know I was carrying. Some things don't come with names, Grandma. But they still arrive, clear as the sky before rain.

I am sitting now by candlelight thinking of a line from *Marcus Aurelius: "Waste no more time arguing what a good man should be. Be one."*

And I thought about *lekgowa* again. Not as an insult, but as a challenge. Maybe I can't change the word. Maybe I'll never quite outrun it. But I can decide what kind of man I become while wearing it. One who listens more than he speaks. One who dances when asked. One who remembers his grandmother's birthday even when we are so far apart.

Her name is Heaven.

And tonight, for the first time since arriving, I didn't feel like something foreign. I just felt…present.

From the noisy corner of the world,
Chris

CHAPTER TWELVE
THE LIBRARY OF MISMATCHED SHOES

Tlhomo's school library was a narrow room tucked behind
the teacher's staff room. Both students and teachers had
access during school hours and simply signed in and out
the borrowed books. Grimy, dim, with shelves that leaned
like exhausted construction workers against their shovels.
Books arrived by boxfuls from overseas charities,
mismatched, aging and vaguely hopeful. Some were
science textbooks from the 1960s. Others were dog-eared
romance novels. A manual on plumbing. Two torn copies
of Oliver Twist. And an entire shelf devoted to poultry
farming.

Chris had hoped for math books. Instead, he found
a volume titled *Algebra for Australians* —useless except
as a doorstop.

Naledi, ever curious, stood beside him, scanning the shelves. Arms behind her back.

"Why do they send us books about birds?" she asked.

"Because someone thought you needed saving," Chris said before he could stop himself.

Naledi blinked. "We need understanding. Not saving."

She sighed softly, her eyes drifting toward the window where students played barefoot in the sand laden yard. "Many students here don't care about books. They come to school because there's food. Sometimes it's the only meal they get all day."

Chris remembered the lunch lines he was assigned to proctor from earlier that week—how they twisted and stretched like a hungry snake across the yard. He had been told by the deputy headmistress to serve the boys first. Just a rule, handed down without question. He followed it.

Naledi stood to the side that day, fists clenched, saying nothing.

When he finally called the girls forward, her voice came—measured, but taut, as if each word carried a weight it had been holding too long. "They think boys deserve more because they're stronger. But hunger doesn't discriminate."

Chris felt it then. A tightening in his throat. A bloom of shame sharp and immediate. "Following directions," he said, quietly.

"It shouldn't be that way," she replied. "We are all hungry."

Silence stretched between them.

Chris had nothing useful to say.

Her words lingered like heat after sunset—still present, still burning, long after the light was gone. He didn't answer. Something inside him curled inward, hollow and cold. A knot behind his ribs, not quite pain, but a recognition. Unwelcome and deep.

He looked again at the girls, still waiting. Some barefoot, some with dresses torn at the hem. All patient in the way only the hungry learn to be.

His hands hovered at his sides, unsure what to do. The authority he thought he'd carried into the yard felt thin now like something borrowed, something that didn't quite fit. The titles—teacher, volunteer, helper—blurred in his mind, slipping from certainty into doubt.

And in doing so, he realized he had followed the shape of a system he didn't yet understand.

Later that evening, Chris found himself haunted by thoughts that didn't feel like his own. It came with the voice of dust and hunger and long afternoons:

Fine red earth clings to my cracked lips. Bitter. Gritty against my teeth. My stomach is a hollow drum, echoing through my ribs. Not the missed lunch ache you read about in glossy magazines, with their plump fruits and glistening meats. This is deeper. Colder. A slow erasure.

The memory of maize is distant now—a golden sun in a vanished sky. Today, only the memory lingers. The children... their eyes are too wide, too knowing. They haven't eaten properly in days. Their bodies are shadows of what they were, snapshots of a greener time. And still, the sun blazes down. Mocking. Unrelenting. It scorches while they wither.

What if the next rain never comes?

The thought claws at me.

A bird panicked inside my chest.

I see the vultures circling.

Not symbols, but mirrors.

Scavengers like us, fighting over scraps. A withered root, a lizard, anything to hush the body's demands. Even the sky seems indifferent.

There's a rumor of aid. A whisper. But hope is dangerous, this close to the edge. It lifts you just high enough to see how far you might fall. When the sun dips below the horizon, the hunger doesn't. It stays.

A shadow clinging to my heels.

Each breath a struggle. Each step a triumph.

This isn't just about food.

It's about the slow, merciless death of hope.

Her words lingered in Christopher's mind, pushing him to question more deeply not just the conditions of life for students outside of school, at home, in the village.

He spent his Saturdays organizing the library. Not to fix it—but to know it. To understand what stories had been given, what had been left out, and what students sought. The books they reach for shape their world. What they think is possible.

Power. Politics. Reality.

One boy asked if Frankenstein was a prophet. Another thought Darwin had been to Gaborone.

It was not correction they needed. It was conversation.

Later that week, Naledi brought a torn novel to class and said, "Sir, if a man can be made from parts, can he be unmade?"

Chris didn't answer. The question was too good.

That night, he penned a brief note:

May 20, 1986

Dear Grandma,

Today I found a book called *Algebra for Australians*, sitting on a crooked shelf beside a poultry farming manual and a love story with half its pages missing. I'm teaching it—yes, actually teaching it to Batswana children under a mango tree that occasionally drops bombs from above.

There is something sacred in the ridiculousness of it all. We speak of square roots while barefoot children chase goats from the classroom. We diagram equations no one here will ever use to buy bread. Yet they come. They come hungry for food and then fall asleep in class.

The head girl, Naledi, asked me this week, "Sir, if a man can be built from parts, can he be unbuilt?" I haven't stopped thinking about it.

Each day here peels something back. I arrived with a tidy lesson plan and clean clothes, and slowly both get frayed at the edges. I am being unmade. Deconstructed not by suffering, but by strangeness. By the quiet contradiction of a library full of mismatched relics, by the absurdity of reading Dickens in a place where children skip lunch because the food ran out.

It reminds me of Ecclesiastes 1:18: *"For in much wisdom is much grief: and he that increaseth knowledge increaseth sorrow."* It was one of the verses you used to quote when the world felt too sharp, too complicated. I never understood why sorrow belonged beside wisdom, I think now I am.

I used to think knowledge was light. Now I wonder if it's more like fire—brilliant, yes, but also dangerous, consuming. What do I tell a child who asks if Frankenstein was a prophet? Do I correct him? Or do I let the question sit like a stone in a dry riverbed, catching light in a way facts never could?

The more I learn, the more absurd it feels. And yet, absurdity doesn't mean meaningless.

I don't know what's being built from all this. But I trust the architecture of it.

Even absurd walls cast real shadows.

Still turning pages,
Chris

CHAPTER THIRTEEN
UNDER THE SUN, A TIME TO BEGIN

The sun clung to the sky, insistent. Proving its dominion one blistered minute at a time. Mid-afternoon in Kanye brought no mercy. The white, blinding blaze turned the earth to canvas, and shadows to brushstrokes of stillness. The air trembled above the dirt paths, wavering like an invisible spirit unsure of its form. It was the kind of heat that rearranged your thoughts, made your bones feel heavy with history.

Chris waited beneath the mophane tree near the edge of the school fence. The tree offered only a scalloped sliver of shade, but he stood in it as if it were sanctuary.

He would've taken off his shoes, but the ground was too hot—even for calloused soles. A bead of sweat traced the inside of his collarbone like a question. Even the insects moved sluggishly, as if the heat had pressed its thumb on everything that breathed.

The landscape pulsed with quiet intensity. Hills shimmered in the distance, the dry air pulling them like taffy. Acacia thorns reached skyward—thin, toothpick-shaped, like beseeching hands. Two Rough-Scaled Plated lizards scuttled beneath a rock, their movements sudden, efficient. A lone lappet faced vulture coasted overhead— silent, ecclesiastical.

The world held its breath.

Then she appeared like the answer to a question he hadn't dared ask.

Heaven walked slowly, deliberately, as if the heat deserved reverence. Her braids were tied back with a faded ribbon, and the fabric of her skirt clung lightly to her frame, more veil than garment. When she reached him, she didn't speak at first. She simply stood beside him and tilted her head toward the tree, as if hoping for just one more inch of shadow.

"You're early," she said.

"I live in hope," Chris replied.

"You live in heat," she corrected, dabbing her forehead with a cloth from her pocket.

They started walking without a destination, westward, away from the school, toward scrubland where thorn trees stitched the horizon and the hills lay like forgotten animals. With the sun directly overhead, their shadows stretched beneath them—thin, sharp-edged, insistent.

"I sometimes think your sun is judgmental," Chris said.

"It is," Heaven replied. "It watches everything. Makes lies hard to live with."

He laughed. "Is that why you wanted to meet in the afternoon? Truth hour?"

"No," she said. "I just didn't want to meet you in the dark."

They passed the wreckage of a broken cartwheel, half-buried in sand like a discarded sentence. Tracks crisscrossed the earth—goats, people, someone else's yesterday.

"This heat," Chris said, "it shapes everything. Buildings. Food. Even language. You don't waste words here. They evaporate too fast."

She nodded. "People, too. You'll see. Even emotions dry differently here. Anger cooks slow. Love needs roots deep enough not to shrivel."

"I like that."

"I didn't say it to be liked."

He smiled. "Understood."

They reached a shallow ridge and paused to look down at a dry riverbed, where goats gathered in the sliver of shade offered by a thorn bush.

Heaven sat on a rock, the hem of her skirt brushing the earth. Chris sat beside her, their elbows almost touching.

"You were different at the shebeen," she said at last.

"How so?"

"Not loud. But… more present. Like you'd finally arrived somewhere."

Chris picked up a pebble and rolled it between his palms.

"I was raised to be still. My grandmother used to say storms have too much to say. It's the quiet ones that make things grow."

Three glossy Starlings fluttered down and balanced on the upper branches, tilting their heads like they'd overheard a secret.

Heaven studied him. "You're one of those quiet ones, then."

"Some would say dull."

"I wouldn't," she said. "Still waters carry truth. But still doesn't mean asleep."

He looked at her—the way she watched the goats, patient, as if studying a family she hadn't yet met.

"You carry your country in you," he said.

"I was born into it," she answered. "But I claimed it later—when I saw how others tried to name it for me."

Chris nodded slowly. "That makes sense. I think I carry my grandmother more than my country. She taught me love isn't loud. That you can care deeply and still say little."

"You say more than you think," she said.

"Do I?"

"Yes," she said, her voice soft but steady. "You notice things. And you don't pretend not to."

A silence fell—not empty, but dense. Something was blooming beneath it.

She turned. "You're not here to save anyone, are you?"

"No," he said. "I came to teach. But mostly I've learned how much I don't know."

"That's a start."

A gust of wind swept across the ridge, lifting a veil of dust that shimmered before settling again.

Heaven shielded her eyes, then let her hand drop slowly.

"You know," she said, "I never liked stories where the girl is rescued. I used to rewrite them in my head. Make the girl save herself."

"And now?"

"I'm writing my own story. Still deciding what kind of ending it should have."

He met her gaze, and something in the air shifted.

The sun still blazed but the shade between them had changed.

It was no longer a refuge. It had form now. Like a covenant in its first draft.

Chris glanced back toward the school, then out across the wide, dreaming land.

"*Marcus Aurelius* said, '*The blazing fire makes flame and brightness out of everything that is thrown into it.*' I've been thinking about that."

Heaven tilted her head. "Meaning?"

Chris drew a slow breath.

"That what challenges us—heat, hardship, even mistakes—doesn't have to consume us. It can become part of what strengthens us. Fuel for something brighter. If we let it."

She smiled, amused, but not unkind. "So the fire is your friend?"

"Only if I remember I'm not the center of it," he said. "Just something tossed in. Still learning how to burn well."

She turned back to the goats, who were shifting under the thorn bush.

"Sounds noble," she said. "But the Bible says something else."

"Oh?"

"Yes," she said, eyes glinting with mischief. "*Many waters cannot quench love, neither can floods drown it.*'"

Chris grinned. "Proverbs?"

"Song of Songs," she corrected. "The love chapter. Real fire is harder to put out."

Chris exhaled softly, the words cooling something in him.

He laughed, not because it was funny, but because it felt inevitable.

"Would you mind," he asked, "if I walked a few chapters beside you?"

She didn't answer—not in words. But she reached out and took his hand, gently.

As if testing its weight.

Below them, the goats bleated once—indifferent witnesses to something beginning.

They sat that way until the sun lowered from its peak and the shade deepened. Until the air no longer scorched but merely remembered its fire.

When they finally stood, Heaven brushed dust from her skirt.

"We should go. People talk."

"Let them," Chris said. "I'll take the blame."

She smiled. "You'll learn. In Botswana, the sun talks louder than the people."

They walked back slowly, their shadows a bit longer now, softened by the coming twilight.

And beneath their feet, the parched earth kept record of the words spoken, and the ones they hadn't yet dared.

May 5, 1986

Dear Grandma,

I'm learning that the sun here isn't just a weather report, it's a philosophy. It doesn't simply shine; it interrogates. I used to think I knew heat. I didn't. The heat here has teeth. It gnaws at your resolve. There's no relief. Not in the morning, not in the shade, and certainly not in sympathy.

And yet—I met her in it.

Heaven.

We walked through that fire today, side by side, under a sky so bright it felt biblical. No big talk, no promises. Just sweat, silence, and the occasional thorn underfoot.

But something is growing there, in the pauses between our steps. Something careful.

I told her about you—how you taught me to be still, how you believed love was like prayer: it didn't need to be loud to be true. She listened the way few people do. She doesn't fill silences. She honors them. And when she speaks, it's like someone opening a door you didn't know you were standing behind.

I don't know what this is yet. But I know how it lives inside me. Like walking barefoot through a land that isn't mine but welcomes me anyway. Like sweat becoming salt, becoming something sacred. Like learning the weather not as punishment—but as teacher.

She suggested we go to Gaborone next week. Just for the day. But maybe also for the space. Somewhere between the fences and the city lights, I might see how this small thing growing in me behaves—under bus fumes and strangers' eyes.

From the hotter side of the world,
Chris

CHAPTER FOURTEEN
THE VIEW FROM THE THIRD ROW

It's often the case, on those slow, rattling buses from
Kanye to Gaborone, that you end up watching strangers—
not out of rudeness, but because there's little else to do,
and because for a few hours, their story briefly grazes the
edge of your own. That's how I first noticed the two
behind me. A pair I'll likely never speak to but haven't
quite forgotten.

Maybe it was boredom. Maybe a flicker of
curiosity. But sometimes, you find more color in the faces
around you than in the land itself, as the bush passes by in
slow brushstrokes.

That morning, I boarded early and sat in the third row on the left, by the window that wouldn't close. By the time we rolled through Kanye's market, we had the usual mix—three schoolchildren with boiled eggs in their shirt pockets, a woman balancing a blue bucket of fat cakes, and a man with a suitcase held together by rope and belief.

And then came the two of them. He, pale and sun-pinked, with a canvas bag slung over his shoulder and dust already clinging to his boots. She, in a wide straw hat and a knowing smile, walking like the bus had been waiting for her.

They sat just behind me. I didn't intend to eavesdrop. But as with all good bus rides, the proximity made privacy an illusion.

Mostly English, but I could hear him reaching—earnestly, awkwardly for his best Setswana. He tried to open the window. She laughed—not unkindly—and said, "Do you want all of the Kalahari's sand in your face, or just half?"

He adjusted. They compromised. They laughed again.

There was an ease between them. Two people rehearsing for something neither of them had quite admitted aloud. A rhythm, not yet danced, but deeply felt. It was clear, even in passing, they were on their way to something tender and inevitable, the kind of love that doesn't announce itself, but settles in quietly, like light shifting across a room.

The bus sputtered forward in a cloud of diesel and prayer. And so we began the slow procession between thorn trees and tar. The way the land teaches you to travel, without hurry, without doubt.

We stopped at places that shouldn't have names. But probably did. A woman with a baby boarded at a tree stump. A young man with a rooster in a grain sack disembarked near a termite mound. Every time the bus groaned to a halt, the white man looked out the window like a student reading a strange new textbook. The Motswana woman, meanwhile, simply waited. She had the calm of someone who'd memorized the journey's unpredictability.

At one point, a man boarded carrying a bicycle tire and a live chicken and sat across from them. He closed his eyes and didn't stir for two hours. The foreigner leaned toward her and whispered something. She chuckled, then said—softly, but just loud enough for the words to escape— "*Marcus Aurelius* would've loved this guy."

I smiled into my scarf. I think the *lekgowa's* name is *Marcus Aurelius*...though, I never caught their real names. But some people don't need names to stay with you.

They shared snacks—she handed him a tomato, which he eyed like a dare. He ate it. He smiled. She didn't say anything, but her expression said, *you're learning.*

The heat built. The bus breathed heavy. Someone opened a bottle of Fanta too suddenly and baptized half the passengers. Still, the two behind me stayed wrapped in their small universe of jokes and glances, and the occasional silence that said more than anything spoken.

And then came Gaborone Station.

The bus wheezed into the station like an old cow meandering home at dusk. Tired, unhurried, but certain. The smell hit first—fried food, motor oil, fumes, people. Always people.

I stepped off just before them and paused, letting the noise swallow me. There were combis packed tight with riders, conductors shouting destinations like street poets. Hawkers selling mophane worms and maize cobs. Goats and stray dogs wandered through strewn plastic bags. A boy chased a soda can. Beneath the pedestrian bridge, a row of men with clippers gave haircuts beside a droning generator.

He stepped down behind me, wide-eyed, notebook in hand. She followed, taking his arm—not dramatically, but naturally. Like she had every right to steady him.

"This," she said, her voice almost lost in the crowd, "is the brain of Botswana's central nervous system."

They didn't rush. They wandered the length of the station, moving through the scene like a pair of dancers who knew the rhythm, but not yet the song.

He tried to read the bus numbers. She explained the real logic—intuition, gossip, and the hierarchy of elbows.

She pointed out a combi half-filled with silence and luggage.

She said, "That one goes to Johannesburg."

He blinked. "Today?"

"Eventually," she grinned. "Maybe tonight. It waits until it's full. Like a parable."

They passed food stalls. She scolded a boy for trying to lift something from his pocket, then offered him a meat pie and told him to practice stealing from his brothers first. He looked bewildered, but he took the pie and ran between the taxis.

They lunched beneath a jacaranda tree near the path that led to the city center, eating fried chicken and talking about things I couldn't hear. But you could tell by the way she sat with her leg tucked under her, her hand resting near his that the world felt manageable when they were still.

And him—he looked at her like a man just discovering the stars weren't static.

I caught up to them again on the return trip to Kanye. The same seat. Same window—still halfway open. The sun fell behind us, dragging long shadows across the land. At some point, she took his hand.

Just for a moment.

But even a moment has its weight.

He looked down at their fingers like he wasn't sure whether to hold tighter or let go, for fear it might break the spell.

She leaned back and closed her eyes.

He didn't move.

There's a kind of silence that doesn't come from lack of noise. It comes from fullness—from the realization that something's shifting inside you, and that it matters more than you're ready to say aloud.

They sat like that, the bus rattling on, the last light painting their faces gold.

As for me, I climbed off two stops early. I had to fetch something for my sister, a sack of mealie meal and a few candles before the shops closed. But I kept thinking about them all the way home.

Not because they were dramatic. Not because anything huge had happened. I'll likely never see them again.

But because you could feel that quiet beginning of a story you're not part of but privileged to witness once.

CHAPTER FIFTEEN
THE WHISPERING FENCE

The village didn't confront Chris and Heaven's evolving
relationship directly. That wasn't the Botswana way. No
one shouted. No protests. But silence in Kanye wasn't
absence, it was echo. A quiet resonance passed between
glances, in the way conversations stopped when Chris
approached, in the way children watched too long.

It started small. An invitation to a local wedding
suddenly didn't arrive. A basket of fruit from MmaPhiri
that usually came every Tuesday quietly stopped
appearing. Chris was still greeted, still respected. But the
texture of welcome changed—less warm, more
ceremonial.

One afternoon, Lesang said simply, "Some people think your story is too short to stretch across skin." Her voice settled softly, a feather drifting patiently toward earth, graceful and unhurried, poised to brush against raw nerves. Her eyes held him gently—yet intently—as if measuring the distance between breath and bone, between heartbeat and hesitation, a watchful grace nourished by the quiet rhythms of doubt.

A few days later, as Chris and Heaven walked past an outdoor butchery near the bus station, two older men stood under the eaves, drinking sorghum beer from enamel mugs. Their voices were low, but not low enough.

"Another *lekgowa* here for the women," one said in Setswana, with a dry laugh. "Soon there won't be any left for us."

Chris kept walking, eyes forward. But Heaven had heard—she always did.

"Tell me." She said to the air, loud enough for them to hear, "is a woman something you *lose*, like a misplaced shoe?"

Silence.

"Or is she someone who chooses?"

Chris wanted to reach for her hand, but he didn't. Not here.

Heaven didn't look back. Her chin stayed high, her pace unbroken.

"Ignore them," she said quietly as they walked on. "They speak from hunger, not from truth."

Chris nodded. "Still, it burns."

She gave a small, bitter smile. "Let it. Fire can be holy too."

Chris hadn't answered Lesang. What could he say to "stretching across skin"? That love should not depend on shade, or language, or lineage? The thought passed through him like a slow wind, warm and steady, pushing against the weight of all the things he had been taught without words, Things passed down in glances, in warnings, in quiet avoidances.

He imagined himself at the edge of a gathering, faces shifting in and out of firelight, voices rising in different tongues, different tones, different rhythms, and all of it—still human. Still familiar.

He remembered a time, years ago, a voice saying without saying: *people like that, we don't mix with them, they're not like us.* And he had believed it then, or at least accepted it, the way a child accepts gravity. But it no longer held.

"There is neither Jew nor Greek, there is neither bond nor free, there is neither male nor female: for ye are all one in Christ Jesus."

The words surfaced uninvited, unforced—a memory from pews and childhood mornings. Galatians.

But here, it sounded different. More dangerous. More necessary. Had it always been that clear? That love was not to be gated, fenced in by pigment or origin or syntax?

That morning, he marked math assignments at his table. Heat lingered in the room like an unsent letter, the air thick with words they hadn't yet mouthed. Heaven sat cross-legged on the cool concrete floor. Her bare heel tapped a slow rhythm, restless, thoughtful.

"You're grading too softly," she said without looking up. "You're afraid of breaking their hearts."

"They tried," he said. "Effort counts."

She looked up then, arching an eyebrow. "Try effort at the post office when they tell you your name is spelled wrong. Try effort when the clinic gives you the wrong pills."

Heaven looked up then, expression unreadable, and leaned forward.

Chris laughed. "So you're saying I should crush their spirits early?"

"I'm saying the world is not pass/fail. And Botswana does not award partial credit."

He admired her then—not just for the sharpness of her words, but for how precisely she wielded them. She didn't speak to be heard. She spoke to *cut*—to test the joints of a thing and see if it would hold.

"So is that what you're doing?" he asked. "Testing me?"

She tilted her head. "Would it matter if I were?"

"Depends on the grade."

She gave him a rare smile, not soft, but real. "You're curious," she said. "That's dangerous."

"To you?"

"To me," she repeated, "and to everyone who wants me to be predictable."

The air between them quieted, but something electric lingered.

"I thought Americans were loud," she said suddenly. "But you—you're quiet in the wrong places. It's unsettling."

Chris smiled. "I'll take that as a compliment."

"I didn't offer it as one."

But she was still smiling.

Later that evening, the crickets sang their silver symphony beneath the hush of dusk. Then came a child's laughter—light as wind through grass. It sliced clean through the stillness of his thoughts, bright and weightless. No calculation, no judgment, no suspicion. Just joy, unguarded and whole. The night stretched wide, stars scattered like questions with no need for answers. And he thought: maybe love was never meant to follow borders.

Maybe love is the only thing that's supposed to cross them.

Dusk came on soft feet. He walked with Heaven to the place where the school fence met the garden fence. She held his hand, loosely. Not in fear, but in fatigue.

"They won't say it," she said. "But they're watching. Waiting for us to fail."

"I don't want to be your shame," Chris whispered.

"You're not," Heaven said. "But you're not simple either."

They stood there, where the goats sometimes chewed on fence posts, where the boundary of school and village blurred.

"It's not us that makes them uncomfortable," she said. "It's what we refuse to apologize for."

Chris glanced at her then. "What did you expect from me, at the start?

"I didn't," she said. "Expect anything."

"That's cold."

"No. That's self-defense. Then you showed up with your long vowels and sunburned neck and you listened." She paused. "I didn't think that would be the dangerous part."

"Listening?"

She nodded. "Men who talk too much are easy to dismiss. Men who listen? They're the ones who rewrite the stories."

"And what's our story?"

"I don't know," she said. "But it's louder than silence now."

June 9, 1986

Dear Grandma,

Things have shifted. Not violently but just enough to make me question whether I'm still standing where I was. There are places I used to walk without thinking that now feel...conditional. Like kindness has an expiration date.

Some people avoid me. Others nod too formally. Heaven says it's not hate, just heritage trying to recognize itself.

She's stronger than I am in this. I thought love would be enough, but I'm learning love is just the start. The rest is resistance, and resilience, and tea boiled too long because no one remembers to turn off the heat. Sometimes I miss being invisible. But I'd never trade her to go back.

We're standing on something ancient and cracked. But we're standing. She tells me the risk isn't in being seen, it's in not saying anything when you are. And she's right. Her voice is sharp when it needs to be. But when it softens, it's where I want to live

Still choosing,
Chris

CHAPTER SIXTEEN
I AM THAT I AM NOT

Mother named me Heaven—just, I suppose.
I never learned to walk with feet held low.
The dust of cattle clung to all my thoughts,
Stars spilled like seed across my sleeping mind.
I came before the flag, before the roads,
before the coin that bore our nation's name.
My childhood formed inside a hut of mud,
with thatch for roof and firewood for dreams.

They said my face would get me what I need—
as though a cheek could purchase me my books.
as if a pretty smile could boil the beans.
No. What I had was sharper than a blade—
a mind that would not bow, a tongue unchained.
I questioned every rule they handed me.
Why must I serve? Why bend my head to men?
Why praise a God who never spoke Setswana?

They named me rebel—yes, I claimed it proud,
for rules were cages meant to trap my fire.
I knew my worth was not my womb or waist,
but how I read, how words curled in my palm.
English, so crooked, tangled up in tricks—
and still I loved it, though it wore a crown.
I studied late by lamp and smoky air,
translating books to teach the ones behind.

I never walked the halls of higher schools—
my father died, my brothers needed shoes.
So I became a teacher, chalk and soul,
a lioness who fed her pride with words.
They said I smiled too wide, I spoke too loud.
I made them nervous. Good. That means they heard.
My voice was not for flattery or hush;
it carried storms, and storms do not ask leave.

A woman's strength in this land is a song
sung under breath, then shouted in the dark.
We hide our rage beneath the cooking fire,
we teach our daughters silence isn't peace.
The men hold court while we refill their cups.
Their ink fades fast, our names gone with the page.
But I—*I carve my name on stone with flame*.
I walk through rooms with fire in my step.

Yet past my door, defiance travels far—
beyond our border, darker cages wait.
Across the fence, a deeper shadow spreads,
where skin itself is judged a bitter crime.
They call it law—I call it blood and shame.
I will not bow to fences forged by hate.
Their chains hang close enough to hear them clink;
I raise my voice for those who've been denied.

Yet nights arrive when strength unfolds in sighs,
as moonlight pours its silver on the floor.
I braid my sister's hair with steady hands,
and hum the songs my mother buried deep.
Beneath the storm my quiet waters run—
a gentle force that shapes the hardest stone.
This softness is my secret, not my shame;
my fire knows when burning must be tamed.

I never bent my days to chase a man,
for hunger, books, and work consumed my will.
The world required my strength, my steady hand,
and love, if found, must find me standing still.
Yet if one comes who sees my soul entire—
not just my face but all that makes me strong—
he'll find a heart that shelters both and more,
a river deep enough to last him long.

I am not Heaven soft, nor sweet with dew.
I come with thunder humming in my teeth.
I do not beg—I *build*. I do not bend—
I burn the map and walk where none have dared.
So let them whisper. Let them shrink with doubt.
Let them believe their rules can fence me in.
Storms ask my counsel when they chart their path.
I am the sky that tells the rain to fall.

CHAPTER SEVENTEEN
MIRRORS AT THE MALL

Once a month, more ritual than errand, Chris Gardener
surrendered a full day to the long, sun-scoured journey
from the village of Kanye to the city of Gaborone. The trip
began before dawn, while the village lay cradled in the
soft hush of dreams, its breath slow and spellbound
beneath the fading stars.

He'd walk the gravel path past the empty
classrooms, their silence like paused thoughts, then
through the school gates, to the hitchhiking spot on the
tarred road's shoulder—arm extended, hope rising like
steam from morning tea. It was a trek carved from
necessity: antihistamines, real soap, batteries that lasted
past noon, garlic if he was lucky and any kind of pasta.

If fortune smiled, as it did today, he'd be alone at the waiting place—no elders with canvas sacks, no young men in button-ups bound for girlfriends and glory in the city. Just the open road, trembling with heat and possibility.

As it turned out, hitchhiking proved faster than the old bus, which moved with all the urgency of a warthog dozing in the midday heat. The bus groaned and clattered through the bush, stopping every few kilometers to exchange passengers. By the time it made its fifth unscheduled stop, Chris was already halfway to the next village.

Soon, he was in the back of a rusted Toyota pick-up truck, wedged between a crate of live chickens, two sacks of maize with a mother and her toddler, the child chewing a toothbrush like a pirate's dagger. A goat rested its chin on his leg like they'd grown up together.

By the time the capital emerged a full three hours later, its rooftops blinking like signal mirrors in the midmorning light, Chris's shirt clung like a second skin, his spine pained with fatigue. But he was here.

First stop: indulgence. Kentucky Fried Chicken.

A relic of home—fluorescent, overconfident.

The air inside was thick with grease, ghosts, and the artificial cool of a sputtering ceiling fan. He paid too much for a drumstick, but the first bite—salty, slippery, absurd—summoned Cape Cod parking lots, radio static, and his father's laugh. Some flavors didn't nourish; they stirred memories long buried under the years.

The taste—something like shame—unlocked a flicker of another morning, more than two years and a continent ago. Same late-morning hush, same hollow quiet. Not Kanye, not Gaborone, but coastal Massachusetts, where the wind off the Atlantic slapped harder than truth.

He'd sat in the corner booth of a nearly empty KFC on Route 6, elbow-deep in a chicken dinner special, a blank Peace Corps application spread beside the biscuit wrapper.

He'd meant only to grab lunch—while the world spun its gray routine. But instead, he'd ended up staring at the questions printed in black ink on government-issue paper, chewing slowly, his fingers slickened as he read.

Why do you want to serve?

He'd brought a pen but not an answer. His handwriting wavered at first—*"I want to make a difference."* Vague stuff. The kind of line high school guidance counselors liked. But his mind wasn't on the words. It was on the booth across from him—empty. On the soft echoes in the restaurant: Muzak drifting overhead, the fizz of a dying soda fountain, a child's laughter outside, muffled by glass.

He couldn't quite say what he wanted to leave behind, maybe the soft erosion of routine, or the quiet weight of days that never asked anything new of him. Some ache had settled into his bones without ever announcing its name. Massachusetts was too familiar—too still. He needed something with motion.

So he wrote. Scribbled until the form was full, folded it carefully, and tucked it back into the envelope. He cleared his tray, tossed the trash, and made a mental note to stop at the post office on the way home.

Outside, the wind rattled the flagpole, and the shadows of gulls swept across the pavement like questions with no punctuation. Somewhere—far away and unnamed—another life was waiting, heat rising off the road.

Now, in a different KFC, continents away, he bit into the same kind of chicken.

He swallowed. The memory loosened. The present breathed again.

After eating, he walked to the President Hotel. A modest, sun-faded block near the government enclave, famous for one sacred thing—cold beer. Not "cool if you drink it fast." Not "less warm than usual." But cold like a metal basin at dawn. The kind that numbed the fingers and made you believe the world still had real refrigeration.

The adjacent outdoor mall hummed with rhythm and color—hawkers trading blankets and baskets, women plaiting hair in plastic chairs, children weaving through a scattering of tourists blinking like stunned moles.

Chris found a table under a faded awning and ordered a St. Louis Lager. The can arrived sweating like it had been dropped from another climate. He held it a moment, savoring the sting against his palms, condensation sliding down his fingers. Poured the liquid into a clean glass, then raised it to his lips, the chill kissed him like an apology and slipped down his throat like a clean confession.

He was halfway through it when he heard his name.

"Chris Gardener?"

He turned. Tall frame, mirrored sunglasses, khakis a wash from surrender—Jeff Stephanopolous.

"Serowe," the man said, extending a hand. "We met in Molepolole. Training days. You were the guy talking about Stoicism, right?"

Chris smiled. "Kanye now. And yeah—I probably was."

They sat beside each other, beers in hand, the mall's conundrum folding around them like a song drifting off key.

"So," Jeff said, settling in, "how's your corner of this African phenomenon?"

Chris exhaled. "Alive. Loud. The donkeys wake me before the roosters. Some kids are sharp. Others, they simply just try. What strikes me most is how respectful they are—teachers still carry weight here. It's messy, but it's good."

Jeff laughed. "Those donkeys, man. First time one brayed outside my house, I thought someone was being murdered with a saxophone."

Chris chuckled. "Still flinch. Every time."

They sipped in rhythm, the conversation unfolding with the slow ease of something familiar and well-earned.

"But time," Jeff said, shaking his head, "I still don't get it because they don't get it. Scheduled for ten, show up at eleven-thirty. It's like clocks are optional."

"They just don't worship them like we do," Chris said. "It's not chaos—it's elastic. Time stretches to fit the day, not the other way around."

Jeff let out a dry chuckle. "Or maybe punctuality's just another foreign disease these people wisely have refused to catch."

Before Chris could retort, two small boys emerged from the crowd by the post office. Barefoot, knees marked by stone and mischief, neither older than nine. They walked up silently.

"*Mpha madi?*" one asked, palm open.

Chris leaned down, met the boy's eyes. "*Ga ke na madi,*" he said gently.

Jeff said nothing. He reached into his pocket and flipped a coin—too quick, too casual. It hit the ground with a flat clink. One boy scrambled after it. The other stood still, disappointment flickering across his face, just long enough for the silence to tighten. Then both disappeared, swept into the chaotic ballet of the open-air market.

Chris sat back. "You could've handed it to him."

Jeff shrugged. "They'll be back in five minutes. You give once, there's ten more right behind them. We're just walking white wallets."

Chris stared at his beer, watching a bead of condensation stall at the rim—like a clock that had stopped mid-thought.

Jeff took a sip. "I'm just saying. This place isn't paradise. I teach English to these people in Serowe, mark spelling tests. I miss real coffee. I miss real food. People who can respect punctuality."

Chris looked at the reflection of himself in Jeff's sunglasses and said nothing.

"You know," Jeff continued, "people talk about how peaceful it is here. But those South African raids last year—right here in Gabs? People died. ANC safe houses. It's not all kumbaya and cattle bells."

Chris nodded. "Yeah. I remember."

"Look, I'm counting the days like it's a prison sentence. Two hundred and twelve left," Jeff said, voice trailing off.

Chris's voice stayed level. "You say that like the country failed you."

Jeff smirked. "Maybe it did. Or maybe I just didn't know what I was signing up for."

"Or maybe you did," Chris said. "But it turned out to be something real.

Jeff stretched, drained his beer. "Well, sometimes real just isn't comfortable."

"No," Chris said. "But real deserves to be respected."

A waiter stepped in asking if more beer was required.

Jeff stood. "Got a ride heading north back to Serowe. Time to get back to the kingdom of maize and morning chaos."

Chris nodded. "Safe travels."

Jeff gave a mock salute. "Enjoy the enlightenment, brother Stoic."

Then he was gone.

Chris stayed. The beer had turned warm, but he finished it anyway. Around him, the mall continued, children chasing pigeons, a woman singing behind a stall of oranges, men haggling over cassette tapes.

He didn't feel enlightened. He felt protective—of this place, of its contradictions, of how it asked you to notice it and not fix it.

That night, back in Kanye, as cows wandered home and stars scattered like broken glass, Chris sat by the paraffin lamp and wrote:

May 7, 1986

Dear Grandma,

Today I saw the shadow side of this work. I met a fellow volunteer—Jeff, from Serowe. We crossed paths in Gaborone. He's struggling here. He hates the food, the pace, the heat. Said he's crossing off days on a calendar like tally marks on a jail cell wall.

Maybe he's lonely or homesick. Maybe the work isn't what he imagined. Maybe he expected something cleaner—easier. I'm trying not to judge. But something in his actions and his words—something brittle—stuck with me. He spoke of this country like it owed him something. Like it was supposed to change to suit him. It wasn't just frustration. It was disdain. As if the place had failed him by being exactly what it is.

It reminded me of that verse from Micah you always loved, *"What does the Lord require of you? To act justly and to love mercy and to walk humbly with your God."*

That's what I want. To walk humbly. To stay present. Not as a fixer, not as a savior, just someone willing to be shaped by the place, not reshape it.

You come to a place like this not to judge it, but to be judged by it. To be softened. Unmade and remade.

I'm not saying I'm doing everything right. God knows I still crave real coffee and lose patience more than I should. But I want to be here with my whole self. Jeff's too busy checking his watch.

Maybe this is what grace looks like—the slow realization that you're not the center of the story, but you're just part of it.

Jeff's counting the days. I'm trying to count what they mean. Maybe that's the better way to measure a life. And just when I start to feel the weight of all this—Heaven keeps me grounded

Love from the southern hills,
Chris

CHAPTER EIGHTTEEN
MMAHEAVEN AND THE FIRE CIRCLE

It was Heaven's idea.

"If you want to know me," she said, almost reluctantly, "you must meet mum."

He thought he knew her through fragments—Heaven's stories, silences, sideways glances that caught light differently each time. But the actual woman, MmaHeaven, was something else entirely.

She wore her authority like the hush before rain—when even the goats stand still and the acacia trees seem to bow. Being near her felt like entering a chapel built before the Bible—where spirits still gathered without pews, where prayer rose not in hymns but in the scent of boiling herbs and goat fat.

Her silence did not compete with the God of Chris's grandmother—it preceded Him. She didn't quote scripture. She was scripture, written in smoke and salt and the long memory of women who knew how to bleed a chicken by its shadow. This was the woman who had raised Heaven—no wonder her daughter's spirit came wrapped in both iron and incense.

She lived beyond the reach of Kanye's last borehole, in a compound where the thorn trees stooped like gossiping sentries and goats dozed like faded prophets. Her thatched-roof hut, round and solid, faced east—toward the rising, as if it, too, remembered where the ancestors walked from. An immaculately swept yard, a single chair, chickens that moved like they remembered other lives.

MmaHeaven spoke almost no English. Chris spoke Setswana like a boy trying to carry water in cupped hands—most of it slipped through, but what remained still mattered.

Still, they sat. A fire between them. A blackened three-legged pot burbled as if remembering rain. Heaven translated when necessary—though mostly she let them fumble in the language of glances and unspoken verdicts.

Inside the hut, on a shelf carved from a single small log, Chris noticed a hymnal faded by thumbprints beside a gourd of snuff and a piece of ancestral bone. The arrangement was neither ironic nor eclectic. It was theological. This was not syncretism in confusion—it was the stubborn fusion of survival. MmaHeaven had been raised at a crossroads: missionary school by day, ancestral rites by night. She had learned to pray in two directions.

MmaHeaven offered food. Chris accepted.

Then she offered silence.

Chris, surprising even himself, accepted that too.

They sat as the smoke wandered between them, curling around unspoken things. She stared at him—no—into him for what felt like the length of a season. Then finally, with the weight of a drumbeat, she spoke: *"Pula e na le pina ya yone."* —The rain has its own music.

Chris repeated it. Badly. She smirked. A chicken coughed up its dry approval, then strutted off like a judge.

Chris nearly laughed. Nearly.

Then she leaned forward slightly, her eyes glinting in the firelight like pools holding stormwater.

She asked, slow and deliberate: *"A o rata Botswana?"* —Do you love Botswana?

Chris nodded too quickly. *"Ee, thata "*—Very much.

MmaHeaven's brow furrowed, as if the earth had shifted under her heel.

Another question followed, this one older, heavier: *"A o rata ngwanake ka pelo ya gago yotlhe?"* — Do you love my daughter with all your heart?

Chris hesitated. *"Ee mma, ke a mo rata."* —Yes ma'am, I love her.

MmaHeaven did not smile. Instead, she whispered something to Heaven—too fast for Chris to catch. Heaven replied curtly, almost like a daughter scolding a flame not to spread.

Then, at last, MmaHeaven turned back to Chris and said, in English:

"Love is not words.

It is staying.

You go home, or you stay here.

No in between."

Chris sat up straighter. "I want to stay," he said, his voice steadier than his spine.

She narrowed her eyes, not in cruelty but in the exacting way a jeweler inspects a flawed stone. "But you will leave," she said. "White man always leaves."

Chris opened his mouth.

Heaven touched his arm.

"Don't argue," she said. "Mum is not asking. She is remembering."

Chris understood then: this was not merely a family visit, but a reckoning. The food, the fire, even the silence, they weren't customs. They were liturgy. Not performance, but participation. He, who had grown up under pews and pipe organs, was being asked to read another sacred text entirely—one not bound in leather but lived in the sweep of ash, in the ritual of sitting still.

Later, as twilight poured in like porridge, MmaHeaven summoned a neighbor. A traditional doctor. *Ngaka ya setso.* He arrived barefoot, bare-chested, draped in leather and beads that caught the firelight like flickering diamonds. His skin glistened with ceremonial oils. His eyes were quiet. Too quiet.

A flicker passed through Chris—nerves or reverence, he couldn't tell.

Heaven leaned in. "It's a test. Just sit."

The doctor knelt and said something in a tongue older than the country, "deep Setswana." In fact, even Heaven was at a loss for a direct translation to English.

He burned herbs that smelled like petrichor and time. He drew symbols on the ground at their feet with a goat-tail switch, then flung bones from a pouch that still remembered its skin. The bones landed with a soft clink— like the sound of a teacup settling into its saucer on a table no one sits at anymore.

Then stillness. Even the fire seemed to pause, as if remembering something.

He touched Chris's knee. Chris felt—what was it? Not pain. Not fear. Something else. A tuning. As if the air around him had shifted, recalibrated, found its rightness.

Then this shaman stood and said nothing. MmaHeaven, watching from her stool, gave the faintest nod. *"Re tlaa bona."* —We shall see.

They walked home in silence. The sky was a deep indigo bowl. Crickets spoke in riddles. Somewhere a dog barked as if challenging the stars.

"She thinks you are still soft," Heaven said finally.

"And you?"

"I think… you're trying. But mum doesn't want you to try. She wants you to already know."

Chris kicked a stone that hadn't asked to be moved. "Maybe that's too much to ask."

"Maybe," Heaven said. "But it's what she asks. Because she knows what it costs when men guess instead of listening."

Something about MmaHeaven's silence stirred a memory—not of a place, but of a presence. His grandmother's Bible had been thick with margin notes and grocery lists. She whispered prayers over bruises, boiled onions for fevers, tracked the moon's phases even while dismissing "all that nonsense."

How different was MmaHeaven, really? Both women rooted in soil, not books. Both answering to the unseen.

MmaHeaven had survived the splitting of spirit— taught to kneel before a crucifix while her grandmother fed the fire for rain. She had kept her gods. And in doing so, raised a daughter whose strength came not from obedience, but from that remembered fire.

And this traditional doctor, Chris realized—this *Ngaka*—was not some mystical relic. He was a steward of memory, part priest, part midwife to the spiritual body. Just as real, just as ancient, as anything carved in stone tablets or leather-bound scripture.

Chris had arrived with declarations, with creeds folded in his *Meditations*. But Botswana's sacristy was not found in pronouncements. It moved in memory, not monument. It did not ask to be translated. It asked to be witnessed.

Faith is not something you hold, but something that holds you—barefoot and quiet, walking beside you like a child, even when you no longer believe it is there. It asks nothing. Offers no proof. Only presence.

June 17, 1986

Dear Grandma,

Today I sat across a fire from a woman who doesn't speak my language, and yet somehow, she heard me better than most people ever have.

Heaven's mother is fierce. Quiet. Unsparing. She looked at me like a mirror held too close to the fire—unflinching, unflattering, honest to the bone. She asked me—do I love Botswana? Do I love her daughter? Not in words. In staying. I said yes. But later, I wondered—do I even know what yes means in a world not made in my image?

She doesn't trust me. Not yet. She believes I'll leave. Maybe she's right. Or maybe she's only ever seen departure wear the face I wear.

Tonight, a traditional doctor came. He didn't speak either. He burned herbs, flung bones, and said nothing. And yet I felt—I don't know. Seen? Measured? Unpeeled? It reminded me of the way you used to pray quietly, over tea, humming hymns that were also lullabies, like you were speaking to something that lived inside the wind.

It struck me, Grandma—this isn't so different from you. Just older. No less sacred. Christianity came two thousand years ago. But the spirits here—Heaven's spirits, her mother's, her grandmother's—have been whispering over fire for much longer.

I'm not here to erase that music. Only to learn how to sit quietly enough to hear it.

I don't know what that man saw in those bones. But I know what I saw tonight.

Love, I'm learning, isn't always gentle. Sometimes it's a fire that asks: Will you stay for the warmth, or stay for the burning too?

Stone by stone,
Chris

CHAPTER NINETEEN
THE SENTINEL

Outside the door of his house near the school, just beyond the concrete stoop, Chris tended a tomato plant so full-blooded it seemed impossible the earth had produced it without magic. It had sprouted months ago in a narrow crack where runoff from the kitchen basin met the warmth of the midday sun, and Chris, amused by its tenacity, had spared it. He even watered it—at first absentmindedly, then daily, with reverence. The plant had grown wild and arrogant, a tangle of vines and bursting fruit, red as prayer candles. It sprawled toward the doorstep like a lover too confident to knock.

Chris had taken to calling it "The Sentinel."

It watched over him in silence. He had protection for it; a chain-link fence around his sandy yard, a makeshift gate secured with a bent nail, warnings issued to passing goats like half-curses, half-pleas.

He did not know then. How could he? That what he was truly guarding was not just tomatoes, but his own ridiculous, radiant heart.

It happened on a Wednesday, which was always a strange day. Too far from Monday's earnestness, too removed from Friday's breathless hope. It was the sort of day that slunk around corners unnoticed, wearing the skin of routine.

Chris had been up before the sun, planning a lesson on solving unknowns that would, he hoped, not cause complete despair for his students. But somehow, the rooster crowed late. Morning light crept in like a finger pointing through the window. He panicked, grabbed the nearest shirt—stiff from drying overnight—and rushed out.

The gate.

It clanked open and stayed open, like a mouth mid-sentence. He didn't see it swing back open in the wind. Didn't think of the Sentinel.

Returning that afternoon, flushed and hollow with fatigue of a teacher misunderstood, he felt it before he saw it.

That something—*someone*—had trespassed.

A black goat stood nonchalantly in his compound, tail twitching, mouth stained with pulp.

The tomato plant—*his* tomato plant—was eviscerated. Vines trampled. Fruit scattered like ruptured organs. The ground, red and raw.

The smell hit first—fermented sweetness laced with something green and bruised. Flies danced above the mess in chaotic joy. A vine snapped beneath his shoe with the brittle crunch of a bone.

The goat chewed slowly, unconcerned, its amber eyes meeting his with the calm defiance of something holy and untouchable.

He dropped his bag.

"What's this?!" Chris demanded.

But he knew. It wasn't just the goat.

It was Heaven. Not *literally*, of course. She wasn't hiding behind the fence laughing.

But it was her, just the same.

Heaven, with her eucalyptus-scented laugh and her hands that moved like doves when she spoke Setswana. Heaven, who once leaned over his shoulder and whispered that tomatoes never tasted like this in her village. Heaven, who called him *"Mistah G'* when she was teasing.

He had left the gate open the same way he had left his affections—unguarded, wide, stupid with hurry.

And like the goat, she had entered his heart.

Seneca once wrote: *"What progress, you ask, have I made? I have begun to be a friend to myself."*

Chris remembered that line now, staring at the wreckage, tomato seeds stuck to the side of his shoe like gum.

Maybe love wasn't supposed to be protected like a crop. Maybe love was the goat and the fruit and the ruin.

He laughed, softly.

Ultimately, retaliation would come, though. Not today. He did not know when. But someday, a goat would find its way into a stew pot. Maybe the same one. Maybe not.

That night he wrote by candlelight.

May 12, 1986

Dear Grandma,

I had a heartbreak today; of a kind I never expected. A goat broke into my yard and destroyed my tomato plant, the one I'd been caring for since I got here.

It's strange how such a small thing can feel like a tragedy. But I suppose that's what happens when you begin planting roots. You don't just grow vegetables, you grow belief.

And belief, as it turns out, is very edible. Especially for goats.

I can't pretend it didn't hurt. I was proud of that plant. It was the first thing in Botswana I'd grown on purpose. But maybe there's a lesson in it. Maybe we're not supposed to hold so tightly to the fruits of our labor. Maybe the joy is in the planting, not the picking.

There's a verse I thought of tonight. Proverbs 4:23: *"Above all else, guard your heart, for everything you do flows from it."*

I didn't guard it well, Grandma. I left the gate open. But I'm learning. Not how to build better fences—but how to try and understand the goats.

Love from the red earth,
Chris

CHAPTER TWENTY
ROOM WITH A BOOK AND A SHADOW

Chris had taken to spending his afternoons alone after
school. The children disappeared in waves—hurried,
cheerful, loud but exhausted, leaving behind footprints in
the sand and remnants of woodsmoke drifting from the
school's outdoor kitchen. The teachers lingered in the staff
room, speaking Setswana with the softness of habit,
marking papers, sometimes laughing over tea.

Chris slipped away.

As he crossed the schoolyard, Naledi and her
friend Neo paused their game of diketo, small stones
tumbling from their fingers onto the earth.

"Going home, Mistah G?" Naledi called, shading
her eyes from the bright afternoon sun.

"Seems so," Chris smiled gently, slowing his steps.

Neo nudged Naledi playfully, whispering loud enough for him to hear, "Maybe he has important business—like writing love poems."

They giggled conspiratorially, and Chris shook his head, chuckling quietly as he walked on, grateful for the innocence in their teasing.

He returned to his tiny house with its tin roof and chipped cement floor, where the walls were papered not with posters but with penciled notes, folded letters, and dog-eared pages. Occasionally, Heaven would leave a cup of tea on the stoop without a word—just steam rising like a question he wasn't ready to answer.

Only three novels lay about—precious survivors of the charity donation cycle. One of them was George Orwell's *1984*.

He'd read it before, in college. But now it read differently.

The passages about control, the surveillance of thought, and the bureaucratic perfection of fear struck him in new ways. He read about Winston and Julia, about their secret meetings and defiance through intimacy, and he saw not fiction—but familiarity.

Their love had been dangerous, forbidden by a state that feared what love could loosen. In a world where

Big Brother watched everything, their desire was political. Personal. Fractured and true.

Chris remembered O'Brien's betrayal of Winston and Julia—the trust they placed in someone who ultimately delivered them into the hands of their tormentors. It made him uneasy, wondering who in his own life might carry hidden truths, silently waiting to betray trust. Society could be its own Big Brother—subtle, watchful, punitive without lifting a finger. And sometimes, in the staff room or just beyond the school's gate, he sensed judgment perched nearby—calm, quiet, content to kill time.

And here, in Botswana, Chris was beginning to understand something similar: that his relationship with Heaven was also seen as a quiet rebellion. Not hate exactly, but suspicion dressed as politeness. Mistrust behind a smile.

Some elders withheld approval in polite silence. Colleagues retreated behind half-smiles and courteous distance, the whispers of schoolyards and silent stares becoming a new landscape they navigated quietly.

Children, however, asked questions with the sort of open honesty adults had long forgotten.

"Why does the white teacher walk with a Motswana woman?" they asked, eyes wide not with judgment but curiosity.

Chris didn't always know how to answer. Not because he was ashamed—God, no—but because the truth was too big for a single sentence. He could've said, *Because love doesn't read passports. Because her laugh undoes my thoughts. Because I no longer measure home in miles but in the way she looks at me across a cooking fire.*

But instead, he'd say, "Because we like each other," and smile, and that was enough. For them, at least. And then they would laugh innocently, yell "*lekgowa*" and run away.

The past, however, had its own rebuttal. The elders' unease had historical teeth.

In the long shadow of colonial memory and missionary rule, skin color still whispered a hierarchy few dared to name aloud. Even here, in post-independence Botswana, the past had its ways of echoing.

Chris leaned back in his chair, the late afternoon sun slanting along the floor through the open door in his house. He remembered reading about Richard and Mildred Loving—how their marriage in Virginia had once been illegal simply because of who they were to each other. A white man and a woman of Black and Native American descent. Loving v. Virginia wasn't some relic from a distant century, it was 1967. Just nineteen years ago. Within his own lifetime. Nelson Mandela, still imprisoned just across the southern border in South Africa, wouldn't be released for another five years.

He thought, too, of Seretse Khama and Ruth Williams—Botswana's own testament to love's quiet defiance. A black Bechuanaland prince and a white English clerk, married in 1948 against the will of both their governments. Their union had ignited political outrage, stoked by apartheid in South Africa and the colonial interests of the British Empire. And yet, it was their love that helped shape the foundation of modern Botswana.

Chris had once mentioned them in class. The reaction had been mixed—a flicker of pride in some eyes, discomfort in others. As if history could inspire and embarrass all at once.

Sometimes, late at night, Heaven would trace the contours of his face with her fingers, and ask softly:

"Are you ready for the silence?"

She meant the stares in the village. The whispers in the schoolyard. The polite rejections from colleagues who once shared hot tea and bread with him after hours.

"I'm not here to be liked," he said once, with a forced laugh. "I'm here to serve."

But even he could hear the lie in that.

There were times when the wind tapped the window like a visitor unsure of its welcome. The tin roof groaned, the world held its breath. He feared she had been anointed for something beyond him—her path carved from prophets' bones, while he remained a foreigner grafted awkwardly onto the vine, clinging to a covenant he barely grasped.

Yet when she laughed in her sleep—soft, startled, like Sarah in the tent—his doubt scattered. A sound born of something impossible, the kind scripture said came just before a promise. A laugh that cracked the silence like lightning cracks sky—bright, ridiculous, undeniable. *"Therefore, Sarah laughed within herself..."*

She never spoke of dreams, but sometimes he wondered if her sleep held more truth than her waking. Maybe, like Sarah, she laughed at angels too.

And in that moment, his heart believed again.

He would find out that his destiny was not to serve from a pedestal, but to kneel beside mystery. To learn what love looked like without insulation—without the comfort of matching skin or stories or cultural shorthand. To dwell, as the prophets once did, in a wilderness not of sand but of silence.

When Heaven laughed—truly laughed— something ancient inside him stirred and said *yes.* Not the yes of ambition, or even desire, but of covenant.

The yes Abraham must have whispered before leaving Ur.

The yes Ruth spoke when she followed Naomi into famine.

The yes Christ breathed in Gethsemane, shaking but certain.

And so they walked. Not to prove anything. Not to provoke, but to exist.

Together. In a place that had not yet decided whether such love was permitted.

And that, in its quietest form, was a revolution.

Heaven didn't always answer those questions. She held her dignity like armor, but Chris could still sense it— a quiet pressure like fingertips against glass, pressing gently but persistently into their lives. And in those hours, as the village sank into sleep and the crickets filled the silence, Chris's thoughts slipped backward, carried like drifting smoke to another silence, years and oceans away.

He grew up in western Massachusetts, in a town where the roads cracked in winter and nothing ever truly changed. There had been one black family in his town, the Davenports. Quiet, churchgoing people who sat two pews ahead in the Pentecostal sanctuary. He remembered being a boy, maybe ten, watching as Mrs. Davenport brought cornbread to the church potluck and stood a little off to the side while the others served themselves.

No one said anything cruel. But no one said much at all.

Years later, he thought of that silence when he stood beside Heaven. When hands didn't reach out. When conversations grew thin. The memory was a thread he hadn't realized he'd carried across oceans.

He closed 1984 again. Thought about Winston and Julia. Thought about Heaven and her mother. About silence. And about how love, in the wrong context, became a question others demanded answers for. About how, in some twisted version of Orwell's words, society might whisper that "love is hate," turning their affection into a forbidden defiance.

He picked up his pen and wrote:

July 3, 1986

Dear Grandma,

I've been reading Orwell again. I know—strange company in a land this bright. But there's something in 1984 I never noticed before. Winston and Julia weren't rebels in the way the world defines rebellion. They loved in a place that forbade it. Not to overturn the world, but to remain human within it.

When Heaven and I walk together, there are whispers. Kind ones. Curious ones. A few that cut the air like dry grass in the wind.

No one says it aloud.

Not here.

Not yet.

And still, I think maybe love, true love, is always a kind of hush-born defiance:

> *Not loud, nor proud—but firm as clay,*
> *This love we shaped with calloused hands.*
> *They say it won't, it shouldn't stay—*
> *That roots like ours defy these lands.*
>
> *No need to fight, no need to kneel,*
> *I choose her still, with open eyes.*
> *Though whispers burn, I will not seal*
> *My soul to earn a stranger's prize.*
>
> *They taught me rules. I learned their tongue.*
> *But never learned to hate her skin.*
> *If loving her makes me the wrong,*
> *Then let the better world begin.*

There's a Setswana proverb Heaven whispered to me once, when the wind was howling and we sat by the fire without speaking for a long time:

"Lorato ga le lebelelwe ka matlho, le lebelelwa ka pelo." Love is not seen with the eyes, but with the heart.

Yours in quiet rebellion,
Chris

CHAPTER TWENTY-ONE
THE MOON AND THE MANGO TREE

It took Heaven two months to bring Chris up to the village
ridge to meet her uncle RraMolefe. Not because she was
hiding him; but because this wasn't just a meeting. This
was the beginning of something more.

They walked in silence as the sun dropped low. It
was mango season and children called out from the trees.
Heaven carried a small gift—sorghum meal in a cotton
cloth. Chris carried his heartbeat somewhere near his
throat.

The uncle's homestead was simple: a kraal, a tin-roofed hut, and a cooking fire where a large pot steamed like it held old secrets.

The ground was packed smooth with swept earth, and the scent of boiling maize mingled with woodsmoke and something medicinal—like eucalyptus or bark. A rooster scuttled sideways behind the kraal wall, as if avoiding scrutiny.

"*Dumela*," Chris said, offering the traditional Setswana greeting.

RraMolefe didn't address him with a greeting, exactly, but said, "*O tswa kae?*" —Where are you from?

Chris answered in halting Setswana. "*Ke tswa ko America. Ke ruta mo Kanye.*" —I am from America. I teach in Kanye.

The man nodded, neither impressed nor hostile.

They sat. Tea was poured. There was no rush.

RraMolefe sipped his tea with both hands, eyes half-lidded, like a man who had already heard a thousand answers and didn't trust most of them.

Heaven did most of the talking. She moved with assurance here, folding her legs beneath her like she had done this every Sunday since childhood. He felt large beside her—clumsy, a foreign note in a local hymn.

Chris listened. Occasionally, RraMolefe asked questions that weren't really questions:

Did he know how to dig?

Did he know how to sit in silence?

Did he understand that love wasn't just two people, but two families, two worlds?

Chris nodded.

Once, he answered, "*Ke a leka.*"—I am trying.

That seemed to be enough.

When they walked home, Heaven said, "You did well."

"I didn't say much."

"You listened. Sometimes that is more."

They moved slowly. The air was cooling, insects beginning their nightly choirs. Chris didn't speak, not out of caution, but because language felt too small for what he was carrying.

He looked up at the moon, resting above the mango tree.

Heaven whispered, "In our stories, the moon watches the lovers who walk without fear."

He said nothing, only reached for her hand.

June 22, 1986

Dear Grandma,

Some days I feel like I'm living inside a parable. Today was one of those days.

Heaven brought me to meet her uncle. It wasn't just a visit—it was a quiet crossing of lines that are older than either of us. We sat under a mango tree near his kraal. A few ripe mangoes hung low overhead, their skins darkened by sun but sweet with waiting.

We drank tea while the evening settled around us. He didn't say much, his questions were tests. About digging. About silence. About whether I understood that love isn't just about two people, but two families. Two worlds. I told him I'm trying. And trying, I've learned, is sometimes the only honest thing I have to offer.

I also realized I wasn't just meeting a man—I was asking permission to enter a story that was being told long before I arrived. One with rituals I don't yet understand, and silences I can't yet name. I thought of you afterward. How often you said that real love doesn't shout. It listens. It lasts. It steps slowly into the places that scare us.

There's a moon here that follows us like an old song. Heaven says in her stories, it watches over lovers who walk without fear. I hope that's true.

With steady feet,

Chris

CHAPTER TWENTY-TWO
NALEDI'S QUESTION

The turning point didn't come from Heaven, or from Lesang, or even from Chris's own troubled reflection. It came from Naledi.

She was waiting after school, her thin arms crossed, her expression was neither angry nor amused. The sun was beginning to sag behind the thorn trees, stretching their shadows across the schoolyard like old scars.

"Mistah G," she said. "Are you leaving us?"

He blinked. "What do you mean?"

"You are looking too far away lately. Like someone who's already packed his bags."

Chris felt it then—not just the question, but the space it opened inside him. A knot rose behind his voice, stubborn and slow, like a root breaking through hardened soil. Not with guilt exactly, but with recognition. A dry pulse stirred behind his eyes, the kind that came just before a storm broke in the distance. His breath shortened, chest tightening—as if the question had slipped beneath his ribs and touched something not yet healed. There was a taste at the back of his mouth, as if a ghost of a coin was pressed to the roof of his mouth. And somewhere in his stomach, a slow twist, like a tether tightening before a fall.

He had no answer. Not one he could trust. Naledi tilted her head, the way she always did before asking for something too big for her size.

"Why do you love her?" she asked plainly.

The question did not strike—it *settled*, like weight added to a scale already leaning. The air around him seemed to be still. Not quiet, exactly, but suspended. Even the birds had stopped calling.

He hesitated. "Because she sees me clearly."

The words felt thin in his mouth. Not false, but unfinished.

Naledi nodded. "Then don't become blurry."

It was a strange thing—a child reminding an adult not to disappear. But Botswana was like that. The wisdom of ancestors, spoken through students. The judgment of elders, softened by the curiosity of youth.

That evening, Chris picked up *Meditations* again. The cover was soft with wear; its corners curled like the ears of a village dog. He ran his thumb along the frayed spine, the same way one might trace a scar. Not with pain, but with memory. The pages smelled faintly of oil, as if the book had absorbed every room it had ever lived in.

His fingers trembled slightly as he turned to the page. Not from cold—it was still warm, the air bearing the breath of a wick that had kept vigil through nightfall, and the veil of distant braai smoke—but from the residue of Naledi's question, which lay upon him like sackcloth on scorched flesh. He read the sentence aloud this time, slower than before, his voice no more than a whisper: *"The impediment to action advances action. What stands in the way becomes the way."*

The words did not offer comfort. They did not promise ease. They sat in his lap like a stone—cool, unmoving and necessary. He closed the book slowly, resting it against his chest.

Maybe the village's scrutiny wasn't a wall but a mirror. One that showed him where the cracks were—and who he could become by sealing them with patience.

But there was another reckoning waiting across the ocean—quieter, more cunning. Not the judgment of strangers, but the uneasy grace of those who called themselves his own. There, love like this would be greeted not with spears but with soft-spoken sacrifices: averted eyes, overlong pauses, blessings salted with hesitation. The danger wasn't exile—it was subtle estrangement. He feared not the fire, but the lukewarm. Not wrath, but the slow withdrawal of warmth from what was once friendly voices. And maybe that was the truer wilderness: not the Kalahari or the thornveld, but the rooms back home where prayers were whispered with one hand shielding the truth. Where love bowed only to a god carved in the likeness of comfort, and difference was an unclean thing, best left outside.

Here, the earth did not flinch. The sand received him whether he stumbled or stood tall. The baobab trees did not seek his intentions; they simply reached skyward without apology. Even the goats, nosing through trash and starlight, seemed to move with the confidence of creatures that belonged. Botswana did not offer comfort—it offered clarity. The sun was honest. The rains, when they came, were never polite. And yet, in this unyielding land, he felt something beginning to yield within him. Not break, but open. As if the red soil beneath his feet had become a kind of altar, and every step he took upon it was a prayer made not with words, but with staying power.

And maybe that was what Naledi had sensed—not just doubt, but dislocation. Her question had carried the voice of something older than her years, as if an ancestor had borrowed her tongue for a moment to remind him: *Do not hover above the ground that would hold you. Plant your feet.*

He closed the book and began drafting a lesson plan in his mind, but not for maths. Instead, he thought about the obstacle becoming the path he needed to pursue. *Marcus Aurelius* was right—don't go around what's right in front of you. Face it and persevere.

But that was philosophy, and this was life. Life smelled of woodsmoke and sunbaked bricks. Life asked questions you weren't ready to answer. It laughed at your abstractions.

Heaven's laugh—yes, that too was an answer. It was not a light laugh. It was weighted, like a woman carrying water in a clay pot, steadying herself over the shifting ground. He loved her not because she saw him, but because she didn't flinch at what she saw. Not the hesitation, not the shame, not the thousand small fears that lived in the corners of his Massachusetts-bred conscience.

Fear was the real obstacle, not the people in the village. Not even his friends back home who would raise their eyebrows with polite alarm. No, it was the quiet suspicion in his own bones that he had stepped too far outside of the lines he was drawn in. That the fabric of his upbringing—stitched with quiet warnings and invisible rules—would fray the moment it rubbed against the rough seams of another world. But love—real love—is not afraid of the unraveling. It pulls the thread with bare hands, knowing that only what is woven again with truth is worth wearing.

He thought about the stares. The low-toned Setswana in the staff room when he showed up to start the day. The long pauses in conversation when he and Heaven walked past. They were not spears, these stares. They were smoke signals. They said: We see you. We don't know yet what to make of you.

And maybe that was okay. Maybe being misunderstood wasn't the enemy. Maybe it was the toll for crossing a boundary, any boundary, that mattered.

November 24, 1986

Dear Grandma,

Naledi asked me why I love Heaven.

I told her: because she sees me clearly. But I've been chewing on that answer since. The truth is, I'm learning to love her the way trees learn the seasons—not all at once. Her strength is not in defiance but in presence.

And loving her has forced me to see the parts of myself I'd rather leave behind closed doors.

I've been afraid, Grandma. Not of the village, not of Heaven, but of what love demands.

Back home, I was raised to admire bravery in war, courage in boardrooms—but no one taught me the quiet fortitude it takes to stand beside someone when the world squints at you.

Fear has a thousand disguises. It dresses itself in logic, in politeness, in "just being careful." It tells you that love should look familiar. That it should fit like a glove instead of stretching you like a new skin.

But Botswana stretches me.

Heaven stretches me.

I think I've been walking around obstacles, and not facing them, head on.

I worried about the whispers in the village. I worried about what Uncle Mike would say at Christmas. I worried if love that needed explaining could be called love at all.

But the obstacle is the way. That's what *Marcus Aurelius* says. The very thing I'm afraid of—being seen, being questioned, being vulnerable. That is where I have to go. I must become transparent, even if it makes me tremble.

Not because it is easy.

Because anything less would be a lie.

So, I'll stay in this discomfort. I'll stay inside the hard questions, the wary glances. Inside the love that won't apologize for being born on strange soil.

Maybe one day the village will soften. Or maybe it won't. But I'll know I didn't try to go around anything. That I stood still and faced it.

I will not become blurry.

With as much clarity and I can muster,
Chris

(

CHAPTER TWENTY-THREE
YELLOW POWDER AND NEWSPRINT

In the scrubby heat of southern Botswana, 1986 ticked by
not in seconds but in seasons—wet, dry, then hotter still,
until breath itself felt optional. Chris Gardener, exiled
optimist, was constantly reminded that time here didn't
care for wristwatches. It was a place of sun-faded
calendars and patient cattle, where nothing arrived on time
except for the sun and, miraculously, his mother's 'care
packages.'

The mornings were crisp—desert air tricking you
with a chill that vanished the moment the sun rose,
unrelenting and smug. Chris would wake before dawn to
the trill of guinea fowl and the low gurgle of his tin kettle
over a flame on his gas stove. The walls of his modestly
appointed four-room government house, whitewashed but
never truly white, echoed with silence punctuated by

children's laughter and the distant bark of a donkey. On the table sat a dog-eared copy of *Meditations*, a cracked mug, and a resolute hope for mail.

Once every three months or so, if the road hadn't washed out, the khaki-green postal truck would hiccup down the sandy track like a hungover tortoise and deliver mail to Tlhomo. That day, Chris saw it before it even turned the bend—felt it, maybe, in his ribs or in the sudden surge of hope that rose like a hymn.

He met the delivery man in the staff room. And there it was. A soft bundle wrapped in brown paper, speckled with air mail stickers like little blue angels. *Christopher Gardener, c/o Peace Corps, Kanye Suboffice, Botswana, Tlhomo Junior Secondary School.* Inside were a *Boston Sunday Globe*, four weeks old, and two foil packets of powdered gold—Kraft macaroni and cheese. Just the packets of powder, no noodles. His mother, ever thrifty, knew the pasta was usually available in the capital city of Gaborone, but the neon cheese dust? Irreplaceable. Priceless.

He would open the newspaper carefully, like scripture, spreading it across the table in sections, adverts and all. He devoured it all. Not just the headlines about Reagan and Gorbachev, but the sales at Filene's, the classifieds, the Sunday comics, the obituaries. Even the ink-smudged real estate listings thrilled him: *"Charming* *two-bedroom, Brookline, near T—$180,000. "* He circled it with a pencil stub, a gesture that felt both nostalgic and absurd. That house could've been a mirage on the moon.

Then he'd make the macaroni. Not in a pot, but in a dented pan with some borrowed margarine and tinned milk. The pasta would be slightly overcooked from the uneven flame, but the cheese—oh, the cheese. He'd close his eyes and taste something synthetic and pure Americana. *Home*.

He found himself thinking of Orwell's *1984 again*, the part where Winston chokes down a meal of oily stew and synthetic gin, a flavorless, joyless ritual of survival. *"It was a dull meal, consisting of a soup, a hunk of bread, and a piece of cheese which was as hard as rock. "* Chris had underlined that line once. In Orwell's world, food was a weapon of control: enough to keep the body functional, but designed to dim the soul.

And yet here, in this dented pan of radioactive pasta, there was pure joy. There was absurdity. There was choice. Even if it was simply processed cheese powder sent in a padded envelope from Massachusetts.

"Why is it that color?" Heaven asked, poking it with a spoon like it might bite back.

"It's…like sunshine," Chris said sheepishly.

"From a lab. Sunshine from a lab."

Heaven laughed. "You white people eat strange things."

They ate it together, anyway, sitting on the step outside as the sun fell like a hammer. Chris read aloud from the *Globe*—a piece about Red Sox spring training, a review of a Woody Allen film—until the light was gone. No electricity, just fireflies and the low hum of cows settling in for the night.

Chris felt it then, the tug between two lives. One foot on scorched Botswana earth, the other somewhere on Boylston Street. But with a belly full of chemical joy and newsprint ink on his fingers, he felt whole. Not divided— just *expanded*. Like a bridge stretching, plank by plank, across time zones and culture and cheddar-flavored longing.

And he whispered, not to Heaven, not even to God, but to the dry, star-stitched sky:

"Thanks, Mom."

CHAPTER TWENTY-FOUR
THE DOWRY DANCE

The weekend Chris sat down with Heaven's uncles to discuss marriage; he thought he was ready. He had practiced his Setswana greetings, made sure he had fresh clean clothes, and tucked into his pocket a notebook full of painstakingly converted pula-to-cow equivalents.

He was not ready.

The cattle post emerged quietly from the bush—a cluster of weather-worn rounded huts and a kraal for the cattle centrally located. Walls patched with earth and dung and thatched roofs catching the sun like scraps of old silver.

The kraal, built from gnarled thorn branches, resemble the ribs of some great wooden beast, enclosing the heart of the place: the cattle. The animals move lazily, tails swishing, their hides glinting in the sunlight like polished leather. Dust rises around them in soft plumes, curling in the air like smoke from an ancient fire. They shift their weight with practiced laziness, tails flicking at flies. From afar, their tails flailed like Irish pennants in the wind, comically out of sync.

The smell was raw and unapologetic—sun-warmed dung, charred wood, sweat, and the sweet rot of trampled grass. Every breath Chris took tasted like something ancient.

Sounds drift slowly across the landscape—a herd-boy's call slicing through the stillness, sharp and musical; the low murmur of cattle as they jostle for shade; the creak and groan of a distant windmill turning like an old man in his sleep. Occasionally, laughter ripples from the fireside like water over stone, mingling with the rustle of dry grass and the flutter of wings as Fork-Tailed Drongos take flight.

A kingdom of thorns and lowing beasts. An amphitheater of sun and silence. It did not exist on any map, nor in any hour—only in memory and bone. Time here did not march. It settled. It hovered. It breathed. Chris felt it at once, the strange hush of eternal afternoon, where even the shadows forgot to move.

Quintessentially, a world suspended in time— where the land breathes in prehistoric rhythms, and life unfolds beneath a sky as wide and endless as memory itself. The horizon stretches out like a faded canvas, painted in muted tones of ochre and gold, dotted with acacia trees that stand like silent sentinels against the shimmering heat.

No calendars here. No deadlines. You rose with the roosters. You slept when the fire collapsed into coals. Nothing mechanical—just spiritual. Time was not counted but felt. It hung in the air like smoke and stretched out like the unhurried tail of a grazing cow. Chris realized, with sudden clarity, that this wasn't a place where time *passed*—it *gathered.*

The place could have looked the same ten thousand years ago. It *did* look the same. Nothing here belonged to the era of ticking clocks or neon signs. Nothing was new or modern except for the dented Datsun truck that got them there, now parked behind one of the rondavels. The only clock in sight was the one in its dashboard, long since frozen at 3:16.

Heaven's uncles—three of them, broad-shouldered, sun-browned, with hands like carved mahogany—sat in a semicircle beneath a camelthorn tree. Their eyes were dark, unreadable, and quiet with the patience of men who measured time in seasons, not seconds.

"Where are your cows?" one asked without greeting.

"*Ga ke na dikgomo,*" Chris said. I have no cows. "Only intentions."

The eldest uncle, RraKgaswane, sucked his teeth with an audible click. "Intentions don't fill a kraal."

Heaven, seated quietly on a stool behind them, gave no sign of allegiance. She stared at the fire. This was tradition. This was Chris's trial. There would be no rescue.

The negotiations began in Setswana. Chris caught enough to feel dizzy: *nyalo, dikgomo, molemō*—marriage, cows, worth. The language moved like river water, too fast in some places, pooling in others. Every question seemed weighted with metaphor. How many cows for a smart woman? How many for a woman who taught others to dream? How many for the footsteps her mother left in the dust raising her?

"Can you herd cattle?" one uncle asked.

Chris hesitated. "Not well."

"Do you have land?"

"Not really," he admitted.

"Does it have cows?"

"No."

Laughter erupted—brief, bright, like a match struck on stone.

They left to confer under a marula tree. Chris watched them go, silhouettes cut against a honey-colored sky. He wondered, absurdly, if they were inventing riddles or calculating dowry rates based on lunar phases. When they returned, they offered a new number. Not in cows. But chickens. Then goats. Then cows again. The line between joke and judgment was blurred. Maybe it never existed. At last, RraKgaswane leaned forward, resting his elbows on his knees. "You will bring two cows," he said. "And you will stay long enough that when people say your name, they do not have to ask, 'Which white one?'"

Chris nodded slowly. It felt like kneeling.

That night, Heaven whispered in the dark, "You handled it well."

"I was humiliated."

"No," she said. "You were initiated."

CHAPTER TWENTY-FIVE
A NOSE-FULL OF BOTSWANA

With the concessions made and the initiation completed,
the sun dipped below the horizon, painting the sky in
flamboyant hues of bruised plum and sunset orange, a
backdrop to the bizarre drama unfolding before Chris.

He stood beside a goat, a creature that regarded
him with an air of profound disdain that mirrored his own
feelings. The goat, bless its woolly heart, seemed utterly
unimpressed by its impending fate, a fate Chris was
equally unenthusiastic about. Heaven, ever resourceful,
had already started the celebratory fire, a cheerful blaze
that did little to alleviate the growing nausea in Chris's
stomach.

The smell—potent. A heady cocktail of
woodsmoke, sun-hardened dung, and something distinctly

metallic hung heavy in the air, clinging to the back of his throat like a persistent cough.

"So, uh…where do I start?" Chris mumbled, eyeing the goat with a mixture of trepidation and morbid curiosity.

The goat, in response, emitted a sound that could only be described as a sophisticated sneer, almost a spitting sound. RraKgaswane, ever the picture of stoic patience, chuckled, a sound like gravel rolling downhill. "Begin by appreciating this magnificent beast. He lived a good life. Now, help him achieve a better afterlife, in a delicious stew."

The uncles, positioned in a casual semicircle that resembled a particularly enthusiastic goat-slaughtering support group, watched with open amusement. They looked like a band of weathered, wizened gnomes who'd wrestled lions and outwitted tax collectors – all before breakfast.

"Appreciate?" Chris muttered, his voice a feeble squeak swallowed by the smug chirping of crickets. "This isn't appreciation. This is, like…weaponized un-appreciation."

He sighed, the fire of vengeance he once harbored for his tomato-thieving nemesis back at his house at school now reduced to a mildly irritated simmer.

He wasn't sure if they understood his butchered Setswana, but the tremor in his voice, coupled with the faint whimper escaping his lips, likely gave him away. The eldest uncle, with an impressive level of unsettling precision and calm efficiency, made a swift incision diagonally at the neck just below the jawline. Blood, alarmingly thick and dark, spurted out in a macabre fountain, adding a gruesome splash of color to the already dramatic sunset. Chris, somewhat surprisingly, didn't faint. Instead, he found himself weirdly fascinated, though the iron-tinged tang of blood assaulting his nostrils wasn't helping his stomach.

It was like a gruesome cooking show, except the celebrity chef was RraKgaswane, who was no Julia Child, and the main ingredient was a severely apathetic goat.

The odor intensified; the smell of freshly spilled goat's blood mingled with the earlier bouquet, creating an olfactory experience that would forever be etched into Chris's memory—and not in a good way. It smelled like a particularly pungent combination of a butcher shop, a barnyard, and a poorly ventilated iron foundry.

"Hold the legs! Not like you're hugging a grumpy baboon," RraKgaswane instructed, suppressing a chuckle as Chris wrestled with the goat's surprisingly powerful limbs.

Chris was having an internal debate: Was he more terrified of the goat, the smell, or the next step, which involved actually gutting the thing? The air was now a chaotic blend of woodsmoke, impending stew, and the distinctly pungent metallic tang of goat blood – all competing with the already existing dung-and-earth symphony.

Heaven, ever resourceful, appeared with a large bowl. "Catch the blood," she instructed. "It's for the stew. Adds—character." Her wink did little to soften Chris's mounting horror.

Chris was now thoroughly covered in a delightful mixture of goat blood and a newfound respect for the animal's surprisingly powerful struggle. He managed a shaky grin. "Character?" he echoed, his voice thick with the taste of blood and impending doom. "I think 'biohazard' might be a more accurate description."

He glanced at the bowl, the dark crimson liquid sloshing ominously within. The smell was now almost unbearable: a cloying, iron-sweet stench curling into his sinuses and drowning out every other sense, now tattooed onto Chris's soul.

Eviscerating the goat proved to be far more challenging than Chris had anticipated. He had pictured it as a straightforward procedure. In reality, it felt like wrestling an oversized, angry sausage casing, its stench overwhelming, like a thousand decaying things. The uncles' laughter echoed across the cattle post like a maniacal chorus.

They offered helpful—often contradictory— advice, their voices punctuated by the irregular thuds of Chris's clumsy efforts. The odor peaked in a grotesque crescendo, making Chris question his life choices.

Finally, after what felt like an eternity wrestling the surprisingly resilient carcass and suppressing the urge to vomit, Chris dispatched the animal and collapsed onto a nearby rock—exhausted, smeared in blood and entrails, and stunned by a strange sense of accomplishment.

Welcome to the family.

January 17, 1987

Dear Grandma,

I just returned from a trip to the cattle-post, an ancient place where I negotiated for marriage using cows I don't have, in a language I barely speak, with men who can size up a soul like a goat at auction.

They weren't unkind. Just serious. Very serious. It's not just about payment. It's about acknowledgment. That I see her worth—not in dollars, but in effort, endurance, and legacy. They say the cow is the currency of respect. So, I promised two.

Yours in bewildered commitment,
Chris

P.S. Oh yeah, I was welcomed to the family by participating in the slaughtering of a goat...I wish you could have seen what I smelled!

CHAPTER TWENTY-SIX
THE WOMAN, THE WATCHER, THE WIND

The vulture watched him.

Chris first saw it beyond the rise, where the tar
road surrendered and gravel took over, indifferent as fate.
The old metal pole, rust-flaked, half-buried in the bush,
and leaning into silence, bore a dented sign with a cow's
silhouette—meant to warn motorists, but now an omen.
Atop the sign, the vulture perched in perfect composure. It
had the solemnity of a priest and the patience of an
auditor. Wings tucked. Neck still. Eyes sharp enough to
open locks.

Its beak, dark and cruelly curved, was made for
silence—designed not to roar or hunt, but to tear clean
through the soft seams of the dead. Flesh parted before it
without protest.

That was the nature of vultures: no drama, no sound. Only the work of undoing.

He stopped walking.

The vulture didn't blink.

He had seen them before—dozens, circling over cattle carcasses, clustered along the bone fields of drought, or pecking at something forgotten by mercy along the roadside. But this one didn't just exist. It *anticipated*.

Chris walked on. But unease trailed behind him like a long shadow with its own thoughts.

At school, the day passed in its usual order: sweat between the shoulder blades, indifferent replies of "Yes, sir" and "No, sir" like a litany he barely believed. The sun turned slow somersaults in the sky. Naledi swept the sand slowly, as if she too were pushing away thoughts. A vulture—a different one, maybe, or the same—spiraled high overhead.

He thought of how much he'd once feared this place. Its dryness. Its slowness. The way nothing seemed to fit American expectations. But maybe that had always been the point. You had to wait. Watch. Listen.

Chris remembered the Peace Corps tag line from advertisements on TV back in the states: **"The toughest job you'll ever love."** It had sounded noble back then. Maybe even smug. Now it felt different. Like an invitation to survive gently.

When the last lesson ended for the day, the sun folded the sky like a letter no one dared to send. He approached his home. He stopped. He saw them before they saw him—two women framed by low light and long shadows.

Heaven. And Lesang.

Heaven sat folded forward, her mug of tea held like a fragile promise. Lesang, by contrast, lounged on his steps, wrapped in that smug stillness. He felt the presence of that vulture again: calm, unblinking, patient.

Some creatures move with silence, then wait for the rest to fall apart.

The bag of books and papers in Chris's hand suddenly felt much heavier, though nothing had changed but the air. He stood a moment longer, unsure whether to enter—or to retreat into the bush and walk until dark.

Chris stepped forward. Gravel crunched beneath his foot. Both women turned.

"Dumelang," he said, his voice unmoored from certainty.

Heaven's smile was present but pale. Lesang's smile was curved like a question mark drawn in blood.

Chris set his bag down slowly, as though it might detonate. "What brings you by, Lesang?"

"Oh," she said, tilting her head like a bird calculating distance, "just tea. And prophecy. I hear that you both just returned from Heaven's family cattle post."

He sat, careful not to meet Heaven's eyes.

"I've seen this before," Lesang said. "In books, on stages, in embassies. A white man. A black woman. A village. A dream." Her eyes bored into him. "It doesn't end well."

Chris swallowed. "You speak like it's a formula."

"History is a formula," she said. "Race is arithmetic. Two races? Add enough difference, and the sum is collapse. You can dress it up however you want— but you can't rewrite gravity." She paused. "That's pure fantasy. Especially when you factor in cultures. And mothers, those are the border guards that history forgot to name."

At that, Heaven uneased.

Chris glanced at her. "We're not a metaphor, Lesang."

"Maybe not to you. But here," she gestured around them, vague as morning mist, "everything is metaphor. Your presence, your silence, your desire. And hers? It will be taxed by customs you cannot carry."

Heaven's voice was quiet. "Tell me then—what do *you* know of the customs of the heart?"

Lesang turned slowly, her voice low. "More than you think." And then added, "Certainly you've imagined how Chris's white family and white friends will react."

Chris said nothing. Because in the sudden stillness, he heard it—the flutter of wings. Not above, but within. A reckoning stirred.

Lesang's words burrowed into him like barbed hooks. Her eyes lingered just long enough to feel like a decision.

Was MmaHeaven right after all? That his love was a season, and hers a lifetime? Would he become another white ghost in the memory of a brown woman? Another promise turned Setswana proverb?

He looked at Heaven—and for the first time, couldn't see their future clearly.

Lesang stood. She brushed off her skirt like she was done with a trial. "I just came to say hello," she said, smiling sweetly. "And maybe goodbye. In advance."

As she disappeared into the dark, Chris sat frozen. Heaven, too, said nothing.

Both completely motionless.

The candle stuttered in the night breeze.

He felt it then.

Not anger.

Not shame.

But doubt.

And that was worse.

And somewhere behind his ribs, the vulture opened its wings.

Later, Chris wrote by candlelight.

Each word slow.

Deliberate.

Like laying stones for a well he may never drink.

January 24, 1987

Dear Grandma,

I saw a vulture on a road sign today. Just sitting there like a toll booth attendant for the afterlife. It didn't move when I walked toward it, didn't flinch when I passed. Just stared, like it was waiting for me to understand something I hadn't been ready for.

Vultures are neither cursed nor ugly.
They're patient.
They wait.
They clean what others avoid.
They don't chase or boast.
They simply do what needs doing.

That landed somewhere tender maybe because Lesang is that vulture, watching for the moment Heaven and I begin to unravel under outside pressure.

Some days stretch hollow and heat-soaked, like a question with no right answer. The Setswana slips through my fingers.

The students are quiet, then too loud, then quiet again. And I don't always know if I'm helping or just floating.

Still, somehow, I feel steadier…a Bible verse I remember: *"In quietness and in trust shall be your strength."* *(Isaiah 30:15)*

That's what I'm learning out here. That maybe strength isn't noise or speed or certainty. Maybe it's standing still under a sky full of vultures, doing what must be done, even when no one claps. And trusting that is enough.

Sometimes I wonder if I'm learning to endure—or just learning to disappear quietly.

Maybe that's a strength too.

From beneath the hush of wings and sun,
Chris

CHAPTER TWENTY-SEVEN
THE STILLNESS BETWEEN THE TREES

By the time Chris reached the edge of the garden, the sun
had already started its tyrannical climb. The sky, bleached
blue and cloudless, gave no quarter. Sweat clung to his
lower back like a question with no clear subject. He
ducked beneath the ragged shade of a mophane tree, then
another, weaving his way toward the low ridge behind the
school, the way he'd seen the old men walk—not through,
but around, as if time was something to be danced with,
not beaten into submission.

He walked without a plan, without intention, just the loose drift of limbs following dust, the way a leaf gives itself to the wind. There was no destination, no errand to justify the motion. Only movement for its own sake. His feet made small decisions his mind didn't question: left at the termite mound, past the thorny bush that always snagged his shirt, toward the place where the sky opened wider than seemed reasonable.

The path wasn't really a path, just a suggestion carved by footsteps and hooves and time. Goats had wandered here. Children had chased each other here. And now he wandered too, with no more authority than the breeze.

He was no longer searching. Not for answers. Not for proof. Not even for Heaven. There was a strange relief in that. To walk without needing to arrive. As if presence itself—step after dust-clouded step—was the lesson.

The sun lowered behind the ridge like a slow exhale. Lilac-Breasted Rollers flew up into the trees, gossiping softly. The air grew sweeter, heavier, tinged with woodsmoke and the quiet music of insects tuning their wings for the night.

Devoid of purpose and in that surrender, something loosened in him: a knot untying slowly, gently, without pain. It reminded him of a winter afternoon in Massachusetts, long before Botswana. He'd stayed home sick from school, curled on the couch under a patchwork quilt his grandmother had made from old flannel shirts. There'd been a silence then too—not absence, but fullness. The kettle whistled once. She had spoken from the kitchen without even raising her voice, and somehow, he had heard her: *"Rest. Sometimes the stillness is the healing."* And now, in the hush between thorns, he felt that stillness again—older, but just as kind.

In his hand, his copy of *Meditations*, his daily dose *Marcus Aurelius*, smuggled into the bush. *"Do not act as if you were going to live ten thousand years. Death hangs over you. While you live, while it is in your power, be good."* He breathed it aloud. It sounded heavier in the dry air, as if the bush itself understood impermanence better than any classroom ever could.

"Is it enough to just be good, Grandma? Or do I need to do something good?" he whispered aloud, almost without knowing. His voice was devoured by the wind, but in his mind, he heard her reply, warm as kitchen light: *"Christopher, goodness isn't noise. It's a presence. A quiet thing. Like yeast in bread, working when you're not watching. Slow. Quiet. Transformative."* He smiled, bittersweet. Her voice lived in breezes and dreams and quiet questions.

The acacia trees cast shadows like broken spiderwebs. Occasionally, a Crested Francolin screeched—not melodious, but blunt, like a toddler banging pots for attention. Beneath the racket, though, a hum: bees, maybe. Or the sound of the earth breathing.

He passed the last fence of the school's garden and stepped into the real bush. No fences. No chalk. No bells. Just thorn and granules of sand and the eerie quiet of a world untouched by timetables.

Heaven.

The thought rose like a flare. Unbidden, bright, and burning.

How her laughter changed the air in a room. It reshaped silence, made it warmer, more forgiving, more alive. It wasn't a sound so much as permission, as if Shakespeare's Juliet herself had turned and said, *"My bounty is as boundless as the sea, my love as deep."* Her English was better than his Setswana, but neither was the language of what passed between them. They spoke instead in glances and gestures: a pot passed without comment, a glance traded at dusk, her hand pausing on his wrist a moment too long— *"palm to palm is holy palmers' kiss,"* he thought, and in those seconds, he felt closer to prayer than to speech.

He remembered the line from *Romeo and Juliet* that had once seemed foolish in a Massachusetts classroom but now rang truer beneath the trees of Botswana: *"With love's light wings did I o'erperch these walls; for stony limits cannot hold love out.*" Love had flown across ocean and thorn, through dialect and drought. And it had landed here. With her. Unexpected, yet wholly present.

He had fallen in love the same way some people fell into rivers—not intending to, not gracefully, and now forever marked by it.

But love across lines—color, country, culture— wasn't romantic in the way his grandmother's soap operas made it seem. It was complicated. Sacred. A slow abrasion of assumptions. Like water shaping stone, it didn't announce itself loudly, it just changed things, gradually, until even your reflection looked different.

Sometimes he wondered if he was becoming the fool Mercutio had warned against—drunk on something dangerous masquerading as sweetness. *"If love be rough with you, be rough with love,"* Mercutio had said, laughing before fate silenced him with a sword. That line haunted Chris now—not for its bravado, but for its warning. That even joy has teeth. That even tenderness, unchecked, can bruise.

And then there was Friar Laurence, cautioning his star-crossed charges with the patience of a man who knew better: *"These violent delights have violent ends."* The words returned often now. Especially when Heaven looked at him with that quiet certainty, as if she already knew something he didn't. As if she'd chosen him not out of infatuation, but inevitability.

He didn't want to become a tragedy. But love, here, wasn't wrapped in violins and candlelight. It was tied up in goat bleats and rationed water and the tired eyes of elders who looked twice when he walked with her. It was real. Which meant it could fail. Which meant it mattered.

Chris and Heaven—no balcony, no poison, no telescreens—but somehow, both Shakespeare's Romeo and Juliet and Orwell's Winston and Julia. Passionate, subversive, doomed in their own way. Both pairs kissed in defiance of the world that made them. But where the Montagues drew swords and Big Brother rewrote endings, Chris and Heaven had only the quiet war of memory, of myth, of choosing where to belong when every map said don't.

He squatted beside an ant trail, watching them carry a sliver of pap like a holy offering. It was ridiculous and beautiful. A memory surfaced: grocery aisles in Massachusetts, thirty kinds of cereal and not a single ant in sight. He remembered fluorescent lights, cold tile floors, the whirr of refrigerator units humming like machines from a distant planet. Once, overwhelmed by choices, he'd left without buying anything. Too much plenty could be its own kind of hunger. But here—food meant firewood and patience. It meant repetition, the same sacred act performed daily with reverence. It meant absence turning into gratitude. It meant enough.

"Don't set your mind on things you don't possess but count the blessings you actually possess and think how much you would desire them if they weren't already yours."

He wiped his brow and kept walking, deeper into the heat. His legs itched. His skin browned without trying. His tongue was dry, and he craved water not for pleasure but survival. But survival, too, had a kind of clarity. It left no room for pretense. Each breath became permission. Each step a small vow.

And yet—this felt real. Truer than deadlines and devices and fast food in passenger seats. Botswana had not asked for his arrival, but it had changed him all the same. It had rubbed off the corners.

He stopped at a clearing where termite mounds stood like forgotten altars. A breeze moved through the trees—hot but honest. *"Everything we hear is an opinion, not a fact. Everything we see is a perspective, not the truth."* "Then how do I know what I'm really seeing?" he asked, his voice cracking slightly. "How do I know I'm not just dreaming this whole damn thing?"

And again, her voice, soft as lemon balm tea:

"If it makes you gentler, it's real. If it makes you braver, it's true."

He chuckled. "That sounds like something you'd needlepoint."

"You laughed, didn't you? Then it worked."

His grandmother had been like that. The Bible in one hand, a wooden spoon in the other. She'd quoted Corinthians at every major crossroads:

"For now, we see through a glass, darkly; but then face to face..."

Now food meant goats bleating under a thorn tree, smoke curling from three stones, the thin scrape of maize meal in a tin bowl. Heaven had made him seswaa once, pulling the meat with her fingers like a lullaby. He hadn't said anything then, but he had fallen harder with each bite. It wasn't just the taste—it was the way she moved. Quiet, sure, methodical. As if preparing food was prayer, as if nourishment had memory. He realized then that the act of feeding someone could be a kind of love too, the kind that asked nothing but left you full anyway.

"But what if the mind is tired, Grandma? What if it's full of too many questions and not enough answers?"

"Then let go of needing answers. Be still. Stillness is a kind of knowing too."

He rose. His legs ached but obeyed. He was tired of being torn in half. Tired of living like a diplomat between selves. The comparisons had become a kind of exile. He didn't want to keep translating his life between tongues. He wanted a language that didn't need subtitles. One where he could belong without proof.

He opened his eyes. Sweat blurred the edges of his vision. The trees swayed slightly, nodding at some private agreement. Everything shimmered. He could no longer compare the two worlds—America and Botswana—as if one were the metric and the other a deviation. That dichotomy was too thin now. Too small.

Chris had once thought, "It's different over here." Now, that phrase seemed absurd. Not because it was wrong—but because it was insufficient. As if you could describe fire with the word 'warm.'

"You have power over your mind, not outside events. Realize this, and you will find strength." He exhaled through his teeth.

He wanted to choose.

Not just Heaven. Not just Botswana. But a way of standing whole, without apology.

As he retraced his steps, the air changed slightly. The garden fence emerged from the thickets in the bush like a ghost returning to shape. The red earth pressed its memory into the soles of his feet.

In the distance, students' laughter. The rattle of a tin bucket.

He tucked the paper back into his pocket, placed a hand over it, and whispered one more quote like a benediction: *"Be like the cliff against which the waves continually break, but it stands firm and tames the fury of the water around it."*

He stood in the hush between thorn and sky.

Not torn. Not waiting.

Just here.

Chosen.

Whole.

CHAPTER TWENTY-EIGHT
THE STOIC AND THE STAMPEDE

The sun in Kanye dripped like marmalade over the hills, warm and gold, staining the red sky as if the earth itself were exhaling. They'd gathered behind the staffroom after a long day's heat—tea, woodsmoke, and the comfort of familiar voices.

Chris sat cross-legged by the fire with a tin mug of Joko tea, its rim chipped like the voice of a long-forgotten song. Around him: Lesang, devious and sharp-eyed; Shadrack, built like a brick and always in motion even when still; John, round-bellied with a baritone laugh; Kerileng, long-limbed and deliberate in her silences; and Heaven, legs tucked under her, eyes dancing in firelight.

"You're always scribbling in that little book, Chris," Shadrack said, elbowing a termite mound of firewood into place. "What's it called again? *Meditations*?"

Chris half-smiled and flipped the worn cover open. The pages, crinkled from sweat and weather, exhaled a faint must of philosophy and desperation.

"*Marcus Aurelius*. A Roman emperor," he said. "A Stoic. He believed we can't control what happens, only how we respond."

Lesang snorted. "You think a dead emperor knows anything about Kanye? About baboons stealing spinach and cabbages?"

John laughed so hard he coughed, then patted his chest. "Stoicism does not keep your tomatoes safe, my friend."

"It keeps me safe from *myself*," Chris said. "Sometimes that's harder."

Heaven tilted her head. "So that's why you carry it? To keep the desert from getting in?"

Chris met her gaze. "Maybe to make peace with the desert and realize that the only control I have is how I react, how I behave when there are things happening around me."

Kerileng nodded slowly, staring into the fire. "You study that book to stay sane. I cook. Same thing, I guess."

They all laughed, a communion of soft voices and orange glow, until the distant bark of dogs pulled their heads toward the school's garden beyond the fence. It wasn't the usual bark—this was sharper, panicked, like the air itself had been slapped.

Then the scream: *"Nthusa! Nthusa!"* —*Help me! Help me!*

A figure came hurtling from the fields—barefoot, shirt flapping behind him, frantic as a bird caught in wind. It was the night guard, Wilson, eyes wide, arms flailing. Behind him, a blur of movement: six—no, seven— baboons, their howls primal, limbs piston-fast, teeth bared—right on his heels.

"Hei, ijojojo!" Lesang cried. "What did he do?"

"Inside!" Chris yelled. "Get inside the staff room!"

They scrambled for sanctuary like children caught in a rainstorm. Heaven grabbed the kettle. John dropped his tea. Kerileng nearly tripped on her skirt but kept her balance like a reed in wind. Wilson reached them just as Chris slammed the door, the baboons shrieking just feet away, claws raking the metal siding.

For a breathless moment, no one spoke.

Then Wilson, panting, said, "I missed the fence with my stone. I only wanted to scare them. Away from the garden. Killed the baby. It was so small…"

"They want revenge," Kerileng murmured. "They remember faces. They mourn with rage."

Outside, the baboons circled, keening with a fury that did not belong to animals, not entirely. The dusk had teeth now. Primate retribution.

Chris looked out through the slatted window, watching the largest baboon—the alpha— sit back on its haunches and fix him with a breath-heavy stare, daring him to blink.

"This is why I read *Meditations,*" Chris said softly.

Everyone turned.

He flipped to a dog-eared passage. "Here. 'You have power over your mind—not outside events. Realize this, and you will find strength.'"

Lesang arched an eyebrow. "You find strength in baboon riots?"

"I find it in not losing my mind when the world tilts sideways."

Outside, the alpha slapped the wall once—*crack!*—then led the troop away, their silhouettes melting into the veld like ghosts retreating into myth.

Silence returned. The kettle still steamed. The fire flickered on.

Kerileng said, "I need a bath."

Shadrack looked at Wilson. "I would not go back to the garden if I were you...ever!"

But Heaven—Heaven only looked at Chris. "And what would the emperor say about that?"

Chris didn't answer. He stared out at the red stained hills.

March 15, 1987

Dear Grandma,

Last night, the school garden had unwanted visitors. Rowdy ones with sharp teeth and no respect for fences. The guard who watches the school's garden accidentally struck a small intruder—just a baby—and its family came howling.

Let's just say I've never run faster in my life. I held my courage like a leaky bucket, barely enough to get inside for protection.

The quiet after was heavier than the noise.

Still breathing, still learning,
Chris

CHAPTER TWENTY-NINE
NALEDI IS ABSENT

I am standing at the chalkboard. The numbers blur—no, they melt—dripping down the board like candle wax in reverse, rising and curling and bleeding into each other. Fractions tilt and fall sideways, decimals scatter like cockroaches, infinity loops I can't escape. The chalk shrieks, a bone dragged across bone. The walls breathe— inhale, exhale—too tight, too fast, like lungs under water.

The air tastes metallic, like rusted tin and scorched maize. Something's burning—rubber, hope, maybe my mind—and the flies buzz, not outside but inside my ears, louder than thought, like static made of wings.

"Class. Class. Settle down please." But my voice comes out thin, shredded, a paper kite in a hurricane.

Where's Naledi?

They don't hear me. They're laughing. Crying. Wrestling. Sleeping. Forty-five bodies jammed into desks too small, too broken. One child is humming something ancient. Another stares at a clock on the wall that has no hands, her eyes wide like she's forgotten how time works.

Naledi, my *head-girl, should be here helping with this unruly hoard. Arms crossed. Eyes sharp as flint, glowing at the edges like embers. Trying to hold the classroom together by sheer force of will. But the room is splitting open.*

Desks groan. Shoes vanish. Socks unravel into string. Pencils are nothing but splinters. One boy clutches his stomach, hollow as a drum. Another's lips are gray-blue, notebook full of nothing but silence.

"We're learning about proportions," I say.

"About fractions. Please. Please."

But my voice sounds foreign. American. Hollow. Like a dry stick tapping against a coffin lid.

Where's Naledi?

The door creaks open and slams, over and over like a heartbeat. Someone asks to go to the toilet, or maybe they said, "Can I go home?" And I nod. I always nod.

Then a voice, not a child's, not even human,
crawls up my spine. A whisper from nowhere and
everywhere:

"You are afraid of dying. But it is not death that
should concern you. It is never having lived."

I turn. No one is there. Just the cracked spine of
Letters to Lucilius in my satchel. The words might be
Seneca's—or God's—or mine, fractured and fed back to
me by the ghosts in this dust.

"What you love is mortal," the voice continues.
"Everything you love is borrowed."

And then: silence. Terrible, total silence. The kind
that doesn't wait for you to speak—it dares you to.

Where's Naledi?

The room stills. The chaos holds its breath. Even
the chalk dust freezes mid-air.

A small child speaks, first in Setswana, then
English. Her voice is clear. Beautiful. Sharp.

"Naledi won't be here today.

She died last night."

And the words drop like wet ash.

Heavy. Black. Permanent.

They twist in the rafters.

They bury themselves in the students' mouths.

No one moves. No one blinks.

I feel the wind leave my lungs, and my fingers go numb.

Dead?

No, no—

Not her.

Not the star.

Not the one who whispered, "Sir, your Setswana is improving," with a mischievous smile. The one who held chaos in her palm and told it to wait.

She's gone. Gone like sleep at 3 a.m., like rain in the dry season.

Seneca speaks again.

"We are waves on the sea, rising and falling. None of it ours to keep."

And I want to scream.

At Seneca.

At the cracked chalkboard.

At the goat outside.

At the ministry that sends half-empty boxes of supplies and full-spined curriculum that no one can read.

At the ghosts that carry off the best and brightest and leave the rest of us blinking in the dust.

I pick up the chalk. It crumbles. Soft. Like bone.

Like something you bury.

I write Naledi on the board.

I circle it. Once. Twice.

A crude halo.

A white ring of grief.

The students watch. Too still. Too old.

One girl begins to cry.

A boy hums again—this time something like a lullaby.

Someone whispers a prayer.

And I understand:

This is the lesson.

Not ratios. Not multiplication tables.

But this: that the world will ask us to love with both hands and then take away what we hold.

That the math never balances.

That some variables—like healthcare, like justice, like mercy—were never factored in.

I try to speak.

But the words fail.

And I look at where Naledi used to sit, by the broken window.

All I have left is this pounding heart.

And a name, written in chalk, that the rain will wash away.

He woke with a gasp, tangled in his mosquito net, heart slamming against his ribs like a fist at a locked door. Sweat slicked his chest, his throat burned, and for a moment—just a moment—he didn't know where he was.

Not Boston. Not the school. Not the nightmare.

Botswana. The quiet songs of crickets. The distant rustle of dry trees.

His candle had burned out. The room was soft with predawn gray; the shape of his satchel slouched in the corner like a sleeping animal. A rooster crowed once, too close. Another joined. Then silence again, broken only by his breath slowing down, one notch at a time.

Chris sat up. Rubbed his eyes. His shirt clung to him like regret. He reached for the small writing pad on the stool beside his cot, the one with corners curled from humidity and age, and began to write by the gray light:

January 31, 1987

Dear Grandma,

I had an extremely bad dream tonight. Not the kind with monsters or old regrets, but something stranger. More painful.

In it, Naledi died.

She's my brightest student. Sharp mind, brave heart, quiet authority. She's the kind of girl who can silence a classroom with a glance—not through fear, but through gravity.

In the dream, she was gone. Just like that. And I was still standing at the chalkboard trying to teach fractions, as if the world could carry on like nothing had shattered.

I woke up shaking.

I've been reading the book you gave to me, *Marcus Aurelius, Meditations*. He said, *"Don't act as if you're going to live ten thousand years. Death hangs over you. While you live, while it is in your power, be good."*

I used to read that and think it was about seizing the day, like some stoic version of a motivational poster. But lately it feels more like a kind of gentle warning: that the things we love—people, moments, small joys like a child's laughter or the warmth of a cracked teacup—are always on loan.

I think we get so afraid of death because we think it's the opposite of love. But maybe it's not. Maybe death is what sharpens love, what makes it precious. The knowledge that nothing is guaranteed—not even breath—reminds us to hold each other with both hands.

I don't know why I dreamed what I did. Death? They say you are every person appearing in your dreams. Is my subconscious trying to tell me something?

I don't know.

I just woke up wanting to tell someone that I love this complicated place which brought me to Heaven.

Thank you for teaching me how to care. For giving me the kind of love that doesn't flinch in the face of endings.

Your desert dreamer,
Chris

CHAPTER THIRTY
WHERE THE GRASS KNOWS YOUR NAME

"He maketh me to lie down in green pastures:
he restoreth my soul." —Psalm 23

It began with a chill. A deep, trembling cold that sank into Chris's bones, though the afternoon air was thick and warm. He was halfway through a lesson on equations that refused to balance when the blackboard shimmered like water and his vision narrowed to a tunnel. He gripped the edge of the desk. Naledi's voice sounded far away.

"Sir? You are sweating."

He nodded, muttered something, and stumbled home.

The sky outside was a soft, impossible blue,
stretched wide like an old blanket, stitched with drifting
clouds and the rustle of wings too far away to see. Chris
walked barefoot through tall golden grass that whispered
his name, each blade bending as he passed. The sun
wasn't hot here, it was gentle, warm like a mother's hand
on a fevered forehead. There was no road. No time. Just
wind. And the smell of rain that hadn't fallen yet. He
didn't remember lying down. Only the strange stillness
that came after the shaking stopped, after the sweat dried
on his skin like salt. His grandmother's voice floated
nearby, low and rhythmic, the way she used to sing when
he couldn't sleep...I will see you in dreams.

He wandered toward the sound, but the landscape
shifted like breath. One moment trees rose like silent
guardians, the next they melted into sky. Shadows curled
around the edges of his vision, not dark but deep. Sacred,
like the hush before prayer. He was not afraid. There were
faces in the clouds, his grandfather's, his sister's smile,
his father's eyes—but none of them spoke. They just
watched, kind and still. He wanted to wave but found his
arms too light, like smoke. He realized then that he wasn't
walking. He was floating, gently, above the veld, past the
cattle post, past the thorn tree where he used to play. His
body had stayed behind somewhere, maybe in the house
with the clay walls, maybe under the mosquito net that

could not keep death out. But here, there was no pain. No
fever. Only the cool hush of evening and the echo of his
name. And her voice. Always her voice. A lullaby wrapped
around him like dawn, carrying him forward into the
great, soft light.

That night, the fever gripped him fully.

Sweat struck him like rain on tin.

His body burned, then froze, then burned again.
His teeth chattered.

But the veld was fading. The hush unraveled.

He mumbled fragments of Setswana verbs.
Marcus Aurelius quotes. Once he cried out for his
grandmother.

Heaven came with salt water and aspirin,
muttering, "Malaria's got you."

She pressed a wet cloth to his forehead. "Sulfur.
Rest. And stop acting like you're stronger than your own
bones.

Chris drifted in and out of consciousness. He
dreamed of cattle taking his math exams, of Naledi
holding a lantern that flickered like his pulse, of
MmaHeaven whispering, *Pula e tla fa o e itshokela* —
The rain comes if you endure.

He lost days. Maybe a week. He vomited bile and
moaned through the nights.

A Peace Corps doctor arrived and left pills.

Heaven stayed.

When he woke properly, the walls were still bare.

The ceiling still stained with rust.

But Heaven's head was resting on his arm.

He was too weak to lift it.

"Welcome back," she said softly.

He turned his head, barely.

"I'm still here."

And this time, the words didn't mean geography.

They meant much more.

February 3, 1987

Dear Grandma,

Malaria is not romantic. It's fire and freezing and losing your name for three days. But I came through it, mostly thanks to Heaven. She never left.

I've never been so scared. Or so grateful. People say illness shows you what matters. I think they're right. I thought at one point that I was going to be forced to leave here and end up seeing you sooner rather than later.

There was a moment I saw her sleeping beside me and thought: this is what being loved looks like. Quiet. Unglamorous. Real.

I came here to teach. But maybe it was destined for me to be humbled.

Still sweating. Still enduring,
Chris

CHAPTER THIRTY-ONE
LOVE AND LINES

One evening, long after the students had gone home and
the candle flame had settled into a sleepy flicker, Chris
and Heaven sat outside the house under a thorn tree. The
night held the smell of firewood smoke and singed maize,
and the moon made the world look washed in old
newspaper ink.

While crickets sang in the background, Chris
looked into her eyes and said, "Do you ever think about
what people see when they see us?"

Heaven turned to him, eyes calm but unblinking.
"You mean, when they see a white man and a black
woman together?"

He nodded.

"I think they see a story," she said. "One they don't trust."

Chris exhaled. "In Massachusetts, I didn't know anyone in my town who dated outside their race. The only Black family went to our church. They kept to themselves. No one was cruel. But no one was warm either."

"And you?"

"I didn't question it until college. Even then, I didn't understand what it meant to walk into a room and feel like an interruption."

Heaven looked away. "I grew up poor. My clothes always entered first. Then my accent. I was told to speak proper Setswana and avoid 'city ideas.' Love was for later. Not for dreaming."

Chris hesitated. "Does it matter to you that I'm white?"

She raised her brow. "It mattered the moment I realized everyone else would have an opinion about it. I remember Seretse Khama. Our first president. He married a white woman from England. Ruth Williams. That nearly tore this country apart."

Chris nodded. "I read about that. He had to choose between his love and his leadership."

"And he chose both," Heaven said. "But not without a price. Some people forgave him. Others never did."

"Do you think we're paying that same price?"

"Not yet. But people remember. And history here lives closer to the skin."

He sighed. "Back home, I think people would call me 'reckless' for being with you. But here, it feels like something different. Like walking barefoot across a field of thorns—aware of every step."

"It is," Heaven said. "For both of us. But especially for me. Because if things go wrong, it won't be you they blame."

He looked at her, heart rising. "What do you expect from me?"

"To stay when it's uncomfortable. To not flinch when someone spits the word 'lekgowa' like it's a warning. And to never, ever pity me."

Heaven pulled her chin to her chest.

He reached for her hand. "I want to unlearn whatever I brought that doesn't serve us."

She held his hand, firm and warm. "Then stop performing love for them. And start living it for me."

They stayed that way until the wind picked up. Not because it was romantic. But because it was real.

May 15, 1987

Dear Grandma,

I miss that spark in your eyes. It's been a while since I last wrote, and there's so much I need to share—things I never expected to feel, let alone try to explain. But I'll try.

Living in this village has changed me, Grandma. At first, it felt like I was walking into another world entirely, slowly, quieter, and deeper than I was used to. The days begin with the sound of roosters, not alarms. People greet each other not just with words, but with genuine time and attention, like every exchange matters. And it does. I'm learning that here.

I've learned to carry water from the well. To build a fire with my hands. To greet elders with respect. To listen with my whole self instead of just waiting to speak.

The land teaches you humility

People teach you humanity.

And then, there's Heaven.

I see you in Heaven.

I didn't plan on falling in love, especially not like this. Her laughter is like wind through dry grass—bright and soft at once. Her mind is quick, her heart even quicker. She's strong in ways that don't announce themselves— like the way she tends to her family or speaks Setswana and English with equal grace.

Sometimes I just watch her speak with the old women at the kgotla and think, *how did I end up here, feeling this?*

But Grandma, I'd be lying if I said I had no doubts. Not about her, but about everything else. About what the world might say, what family might say. We come from such different places, different pasts, different paths.

I wonder if love is enough to carry all that weight. And yet, something in me: maybe this is the truest kind of love—the one that crosses lines, not because it ignores them, but because it chooses to move through them, honestly.

I guess I'm writing not just to tell you, but to ask if a person ever falls in love in a way that doesn't make sense on paper, but makes perfect sense in your soul?

I think you'd understand. I miss your steady way of knowing. I hope I'm changing in a way that you'd be proud of.

With love in what I am becoming,
Chris

CHAPTER THIRTY-TWO
IF YOU PULL THAT THREAD

Earlier that day, as Chris walked through the market, a villager had stared openly, then muttered something sharp in Setswana. Chris caught the word *lekgowa*—white person—and the sideways glance that followed felt heavier than the word itself.

He expected it but hoped he'd have one day in the village without it. *Lekgowa*. Not out here, not beneath this endless sky, with the sun stretching shadows over the cracked earth and the air steeped in the scent of red clay, mopane, and sun-warmed grass.

The group stood in a loose circle near the trucks, the kind of casual village gathering that should have felt easy. Someone laughed, someone passed a bottle, and then—there it was again. The word. Cutting and offhand, tossed into the open like it meant nothing.

But it did matter. It hit him hard this time—clean and sudden, like a stone to the ribs. For a second, he just stood there, blinking, the words hung like a storm cloud overhead. Had he heard it yet again? *Lekgowa.* The smirk that followed said yes. Said *you know exactly what you heard.* No one else flinched. The laughter continued, just a beat too long. The circle held.

Something twisted inside him this time. A quiet tension curled in his chest, spreading like cold water. He forced a smile—small, tight, wrong—and swallowed a thousand things he wanted to say. He felt his skin suddenly too visible, like he'd been placed under a lens and dissected, reduced to a punchline wrapped in a stereotype. His hands balled up in his pockets, every muscle taut with restraint. He wanted to vanish. Or explode. A foreign man in a foreign land, parsing nuances he barely grasped, clutching his emotions like contraband.

You can only truly control how you react, he told himself.

They kept talking. He stopped listening.

The wind clawed at his boots, stirring the brittle ground like a warning. The grasses rustled dryly. The horizon stretched out in silence, and for a moment he let his gaze drift there—to that endless, open space. Then came the anger. Not loud or reckless. Controlled. Heavy. The kind of anger that simmers low, then coils tight in the gut like a clenched fist. He couldn't stay. Not here.

Control yourself!

Without a word, he turned and walked away. The sound of his boots crunching over dry ground was the only goodbye. Behind him, voices dimmed and then faded.

The sky above him was clear, its deep blue hue echoing a color on the Botswana flag, but the weight in his chest didn't lift. It stayed there—real, unresolved. He didn't have the words yet, not the ones sharp enough to cut through ignorance and land clean.

Heaven had just come back from Gaborone. Chris from the market. They sat under the tree outside his house. The light thinned into gold threads, pulling shadows long and daggered across the earth.

"You've been quiet," Chris said.

Heaven didn't answer. She picked at the edge of her shawl, her fingers tracing frayed threads. When she finally spoke, it wasn't a question.

"She said it wouldn't last."

Chris blinked. "Who?"

"Lesang."

He exhaled slowly. "Are you really bringing her into this?"

"She's already in it," Heaven said. "You just don't see her. Not the way I do. She's not watching you. She's *waiting* for me to be right. About you."

"I didn't do anything wrong."

"You don't have to. That's the prediction, Chris. That's the whole point." Her voice was quiet, but firm. "She said it would crack without anyone meaning to. That we would try and still fail. That race, culture, and the weight of the world would bend us. That eventually, you'd go back to a place where I couldn't follow."

She didn't finish. She looked away.

"You're not saying you believe her."

"I'm saying I heard the word *lekgoa* before you told me. I know what it does to you. I saw your eyes when you came home. I saw the part of you that wanted to run."

"That's not what I felt."

"Isn't it?"

Chris paused. The silence filled the space between them like rising floodwater. He reached for Setswana, desperate to bridge the gap.

"Ke batla go utlwa," he said.

Heaven's eyes narrowed. "You meant to say you want to understand. But you just said you want to be heard. Again."

His mouth opened, then closed.

Utlwa.

Tlhaloganya.

Utlwa can mean hear, feel, or understand depending on context. While *tlhaloganya* refers to deep comprehension. Listening is the first step. Understanding goes further. Setswana can be tricky—especially when emotions run hot.

He knew the difference. He just chose the wrong Setswana word. Again.

Chris should have just stuck to his mother tongue.

"You think I've changed?" he asked.

"No," she said. "I think you've split. One part of you is still trying to love this place. The other is already walking away from it."

"That's not fair—"

"It's not about fairness. It's about truth. And the truth is, Lesang does not hover—she circles, low and knowing, as those sent to witness the fall. Perhaps she sees what we deny. Perhaps she waits, not to warn, but to watch the prophecy complete itself."

Chris stood. His mouth was dry. "You said you trusted me."

"I did." Her voice cracked slightly. "But now I feel like I'm holding something that's already started to break."

A pause. Then: "If this is what love looks like," she whispered, "maybe it's not enough."

She walked away.

Her shawl fluttered like a torn flag.

Her steps were soft.

Final.

His words hung heavy with regret, echoing the widening chasm. The land, harsh and unforgiving, mirrored their fractured connection. Self-doubt gnawed at him; was his love inadequate, was it his love failing, or was it the land itself that tested all tenderness? The weight of what was unspoken pressed down.

The words exchanged. A grotesque, shimmering jellyfish of my own making. A fracturing of something fundamental. It wasn't just a misplaced adjective, a clumsy phrase; it was a seismic shift in the fabric of reality itself, a tear in the veil separating this mundane existence from the whispering chaos beyond.

Her eyes, usually pools of quiet understanding, are now galaxies swirling with a cold, distant light... are they even *her* eyes anymore? Or are they windows into a dimension where the consequences of my words are already playing out, a terrifying, accelerated timeline where everything I hold dear is consumed by an inevitable entropy?

This isn't regret. This is a visceral awareness of causal links stretching out impossibly far. A web of interconnectedness so vast it threatens to unravel the very concept of 'self'. My breath hitches, not from fear, but from the sheer, suffocating weight of this... responsibility.

A responsibility that extends beyond her, beyond the immediate, into a multiversal tapestry I never even knew existed, where every syllable is a brushstroke on a canvas of eternity. This silence isn't just the absence of sound; it's the deafening roar of infinite possibilities collapsing into a single, agonizing present. The air itself feels thick, iridescent, like oil on water, reflecting distorted images of what could have been, what *should* have been, and what now – terrifyingly – *is*.

Is that... forgiveness? Or is it something far more sinister, a claim upon my soul, a consequence woven into the very laws of the universe, a price to be paid in a currency I don't even comprehend? I can feel the threads pulling, unraveling the carefully constructed narrative of my life, the illusion of control dissolving into the chaotic beauty of a reality far beyond my meager understanding.

He clung to his grandmother's wisdom, a lifeline in this turbulent sea of emotions, hoping forgiveness, not forgetting, would bridge the distance.

It had to be more than a single, ill-chosen word. It felt like a curse summoned by the misunderstanding itself.

There was nothing left to say aloud. But there was always the page.

That night, Chris wrote:

September 1, 1987

Dear Grandma,

I said something wrong, or maybe I didn't say enough.

Back in Molepolole, during training, they told us culture was like an iceberg—mostly hidden—but no one warned me how sharp the part below the surface could be, or how easily it could pierce the man I thought I was becoming.

There's a distance between me and Heaven, and I don't know if it's mine, or hers, or something the land itself made. Maybe it's both. Maybe all love is partly built from the walls we don't know we're laying.

Maybe she was right—Lesang, I mean. Not about us breaking, but about how easy it is to start splitting in small, invisible ways.

Maybe all love is built on ground we don't fully know, and we lay bricks without meaning to; out of habit, out of fear, to protect the very thing we might be burying.

You always said love was patient. But patience is easier in quiet rooms, not ones full of jealousy and exclusion.

But I remember what you told me once: Forgiveness is not forgetting. It's choosing not to use the memory as a weapon. I hope I can learn that here.

With hope from this place of silence,
Chris

CHAPTER THIRTY-THREE
WHAT THE SILENCE HOLDS

The morning after the argument, Chris woke even before the cooing of the Cape turtle doves. The sky had barely lifted from its blanket of stars when he stepped outside.

In Botswana, some say night is not darkness, but an old blanket the ancestors pull over the world to let it rest. The stars are pinpricks worn through the fabric by time, little holes where sunlight still leaks in. Chris liked that. It meant even in the deepest night, the day was still trying. It meant nothing ever vanishes, merely waits.

The air was cool, the village still. He didn't sleep much, though his body ached for it.

Heaven hadn't returned.

He went to school, taught with distracted precision, nodded through conversations, and eluded

Lesang's hovering. The question in her eyes hung there; uninvited and unspoken, quiet, exact, and waiting for something to die before it could be voiced.

He gave some cursory answers to Naledi's typical clever inquiries. The hours ticked by like uneven footsteps.

That evening, he found himself walking the old path past the edge of Kanye, the one that led toward the open ridge. Toward her. No plan. Just a heaviness in his feet that only movement might relieve.

Heaven was sitting beneath the mango tree. The same place as weeks before. She looked up when she heard him. Didn't smile. But didn't turn away, either.

"I didn't know if you'd come," she said.

"I didn't either," he replied.

They sat for a long while in silence, which was no longer thick with anger, but brittle with possibility.

He spoke first. "I want to say sorry. Not because I think I was wrong. But because I don't want to be right if it means being alone. I carried too much into yesterday. And I let it speak."

Chris wanted to mention the latest *lekgowa* remark. But today wasn't for explaining or justifying. Just healing.

Heaven's eyes narrowed, as if peering through him.

"You're trying," she said. "But I'm not a mountain you climb just to feel taller. I'm a woman. I want to be seen from the ground."

"I know."

"No," she said gently. "You're learning. That's different."

Another silence passed. A goat bleated in the distance. A rooster, confused, squawked though it was not yet dusk.

"I still want this," Chris said finally. "Us. Even if I get it wrong sometimes."

Heaven looked away, then back. "Then stay. But not just in body. In heart. In hunger. In listening."

He nodded.

They didn't touch.

Not yet.

But something had returned.

A thread once unraveled and torn, now re-tied with trembling hands.

September 5, 1987

Dear Grandma,

There were words between us. Spoken too fast and understood too late. Heaven and me. It wasn't shouting, but it was sharp. I've never had someone hold me accountable with so few words.

She's not afraid of truth.

I think she expects it from me now, too.

We sat together again today. It's not fixed. But it's not broken either.

We're somewhere in between. Like the moon before it's full. There's more to come. I think that's what forgiveness is—a choice to wait for more.

You always said love was like tending to a fire. Not the heat.

But the tending. I understand that now.

With hopefulness and matches,
Chris

CHAPTER THIRTY-FOUR
UNCLE THUSO'S VISIT

The clatter of mismatched sandals echoed down the sun-cracked path long before the man appeared. It was a sound like drunken maracas—loud, offbeat, and vaguely threatening. He emerged at the edge of the yard like an apparition that had bargained with several storms and lost.

He walked like a man trying not to fall off the earth—zigzagging, humming tunelessly, and cradling a bottle wrapped in a brown cloth that had long since given up pretending to be discreet. The kind of cloth that once held peaches. Or a dead bird. Or both.

"Ke mongwe wa lesika!" he slurred. "I am one of your relatives!"

His arms flung wide like he was trying to hug the entire horizon.

Heaven sighed with her entire body and closed her eyes. "Thuso."

Chris blinked. "Friend of yours?"

"My grandmother's brother's son. Uncle, technically. By blood, by volume, and by sheer velocity of chaos."

Heaven added dryly, "Remember what I told you about extended family here—there's no such thing as too distant. If you shared a cup of tea with someone's cousin in 1963, you might be expected to help build their house."

Thuso stumbled through the gate like he owned the land and had possibly misplaced it somewhere nearby. He reeked faintly of sweat and something that might've been low tide if Botswana weren't landlocked.

He seized Chris's hand in a grip that might have been affectionate or just structurally unsound, shaking it with the force of a washing machine on spin cycle.

"I heard you're marrying Heaven!" Thuso grinned, his bloodshot eyes suddenly steady, as if seeing beyond the present. "Good. Marrying a Mabono woman is like marrying the moon—she rises on her own time, answers to no man, and carries the power to shape oceans and destinies alike."

Chris tried not to laugh. Heaven looked away.

Thuso dropped into a plastic chair like it was a throne. He unslung a wooden pipe from his shirt pocket like a magician producing a rabbit, then gestured vaguely to the bottle.

"You know," he said, lighting the pipe with the grace of a sleepy porcupine, "the problem with white men is not that they're white. It's that they think they're guests. But guests don't marry the host's daughter." He took a long swig of the Four Roses whiskey. "You, my pale friend, are no longer a guest. You are the goat who stayed after the feast."

Chris opened his mouth to respond, then thought better of it.

They gathered around the fire that night, with leftover chicken from lunch sizzling on the braai and Thuso expounding loudly on everything from marriage to mythology to the mechanics of digestion.

"There was a baboon priest in Serowe once," Thuso declared. "Married seven women. All of them still waiting for him to come back from the bush."

Heaven, now peeling a mango with clinical detachment, muttered, "That story changes every year."

"Good stories *should* evolve!" Thuso bellowed. "Like marriages. Or shoes. Or soup."

At some point, he trailed off mid-rant about donkeys with political ambitions and collapsed with his head nestled lovingly against a crate of onions, snoring like a broken accordion.

Chris looked at Heaven through the dancing firelight. "Is he always like this?"

"No," she said. "Sometimes he's worse."

They both laughed, the kind of laughter that arrives not with punchlines, but with relief. And in that ludicrousness—in onion pillows and lunar compliments and the sheer unpredictability of this country—Chris felt something inside him stretch and release. Like a knot in his chest becoming a string that hummed with a tune he didn't know he needed.

Thuso snored.

The fire crackled.

And for one evening, the world didn't weigh quite so heavily.

September 3, 1987

Dear Grandma,

I write today thinking about how I always picture you— wrapped in a knitted shawl, a cup of tea gone lukewarm beside the window, and four cards away from declaring victory at bridge.

It's been a whirlwind here in Botswana. Just when I think I've learned the rhythm of things, the country throws me a new drumbeat.

Recently, I met more of Heaven's extended family— though "extended" hardly captures it. They flow in and out of each other's homes like rainwater in the dry season. I met her great-aunt who still carries firewood on her head at seventy. Her second cousin repairs tire punctures near one of the markets. And then there was Uncle Thuso.

Heaven warned me, but I was not prepared.

He arrived unannounced, half-drunk declaring himself a prophet, a philosopher, and a barbecue enthusiast in the same sentence. He gave me marital advice and told stories about baboons with wedding rings. He may have insulted me, blessed me, and unofficially adopted me, all in the same breath.

But here's what struck me most: no one questioned his place. No one rolled their eyes or asked why he came. He belonged. Even in his madness, even when passed out on a crate of onions, he belonged.

It made me think of our own family, birthdays and Christmas are sometimes the only glue. How distance, both physical and emotional, becomes normal. We say "nuclear family" like it's a strength, but sometimes it feels like we've split the atom too far, left only sparks where warmth used to be.

Here, family isn't a concept you outgrow. It's a web you stay woven into, no matter how loud, drunk, or inconvenient the thread might be. There's something beautiful in that chaos. Something ancient.

Anyway, the roosters are screeching, and the sun is setting in burnt-orange bruises and Heaven just called me to come stir the pot.

Woven in and wonderfully out of my depth,
Chris

CHAPTER THIRTY-FIVE
THE MEMORY OF WATER

The air smelled like struck iron—lightning, somewhere
near but withheld. Over the ridge, the clouds curled
inward, dark, like secrets not yet ready to speak. Chris sat
on the staff room steps, elbows on his knees, watching the
sky's elaborate pretense.

It had been like this for days. Heat rising from the
dust in silent columns, blurring the horizon. Wind that
teased but never stayed. The sky had become an unfaithful
friend—full of noise, void of promise.

He didn't notice Heaven until she was beside him,
barefoot and quiet, balancing a mango in one hand, a bowl
in the other, a tin spoon tucked into the folds of her skirt.
She offered him the bowl. He took it without words. The

sour milk clung to his throat, but the texture of pap grounded him.

"Still dry," he said, nodding toward the sky.

Heaven followed his gaze. "Always the same dance," she replied. "The clouds rehearse. The land listens. And then—nothing."

A gust of wind kicked through the schoolyard, plucking test papers from his lap. They lifted like startled birds, wheeling briefly before settling in the dirt. One caught in a thorn bush and fluttered there like a captured prayer. The papers lay everywhere like offerings the wind had misplaced—resting on stone, thorn, and dry grass as if waiting to be read by something older than men.

Chris made no move to retrieve them. He only watched, as if his stillness might call them back.

"I keep waiting," he said. "For something. A sign. A clearing."

She didn't answer right away. Instead, she reached into her pocket and handed him a folded cloth. He pressed it to his forehead. The sweat was constant now, but no longer urgent. Just salt. Just time.

He spoke again, softer. "I don't even know what I'm waiting for anymore."

"You think the earth waits?" she asked. "You think it stares up at the sky like this, wondering if it's done something wrong?"

"The earth knows more than I do, I think."

She smiled faintly. "Rain doesn't fall because it's owed. It falls because the roots remember how to ask for it."

Inside the staff room, Lesang laughed. That sound—once warm, once something he followed without thinking—passed through him like wind through cracked windows. Not cold. Just gone. It echoed like laughter from the Book of Lamentations—dry, distant, and meant for ruins. As if some wilderness spirit were keeping tally of the fallen.

Two boys ran across the yard, kicking up sand and shouting, "Mistah G! *Mmolai wa dipalo!*"—killer of numbers. Chris lifted a hand in mock surrender. The boys cackled and disappeared into the garden behind the water tank.

He looked down at his feet, then at hers. Her toes were streaked with a light coating of red earth, the curve of her ankle lit by a sliver of late sun. He wanted to say something kind, something human, but the moment at hand didn't ask for it.

"You ever think signs don't come down at all?" she said.

He raised his eyes.

"Maybe they grow," she continued. "Like okra. Like bones. Maybe they start beneath you, not above."

He turned that over. "So, I shouldn't wait?"

"Wait, but differently."

"Differently?"

"Don't wait like the sky owes you something. Wait like the earth—quiet, patient, full of its own questions."

They sat in silence for a moment. A bird called twice from the fig tree near the outhouses. Then again, as if to confirm itself.

"I read something once," he said. "*Marcus Aurelius*. Roman emperor. Philosopher. He wrote: *'Don't waste time thinking about what a good man should be. Be one.'*"

Heaven raised an eyebrow. "Is that a challenge?"

"Maybe."

"You want to be a good man?"

He looked at her then—really looked.

At the dust along her collarbone.

The way the light curved across her cheek,

The faint line on her brow that appeared only when she was fully serious.

"I want to be a better one," he said.

Heaven looked directly into his eyes and said, "then start there and don't ask the rain to clean you first."

She stood, brushing the folds of her skirt. "Come," she said. "Let's gather your test papers before the goats find them."

He hesitated.

"Or do you plan to let the answers fly away?"

Chris smiled. "Maybe some answers are better that way."

She stepped into the yard and began collecting the pages. He followed.

As they worked, the sky shifted again. The clouds began to stretch, their bellies tinged with faint copper, like old coins warming in a child's pocket. Not a storm, not yet. But something was moving. A rumor of rain.

They met in the middle of the yard. She handed him a sheet. "This one's got a perfect score," she said. "Maybe you're not such a killer after all."

"Or maybe I'm learning which numbers matter."

Later that night, Chris sat alone at his desk, the paraffin lamp beside him, its light soft and flickering. The walls exhaled with heat. His pen hovered above the page, uncertain.

He thought of Grandma—her voice, her garden, the way she used to say, *"The plants don't grow because you stand over them. They grow when they're not looking at you."*

He wrote slowly, deliberately, a single line across the paper:

The rain didn't come, but the earth remembered its thirst.

He left it there. No full letter today. No explanation. Some truths needed only to be witnessed.

Outside, the sky pulsed with distant heat lightning.

And somewhere, under the crust of sleeping soil, the roots waited.

Not in panic,

Not in despair.

But in faith.

In silence.

In the steady memory of water.

CHAPTER THIRTY-SIX
AFTER THE STORM

The rain finally came. After weeks of oppressive heat and silent skies, the clouds opened with the force of a long-held breath. Chris watched from the shelter of the school porch, actually a roof overhang, captivated by the sheets of water pounding the dry earth, turning dust into rivers of muddy promise.

Chris had heard the word *pula* a hundred times before he understood it. At first, he thought it meant rain—just rain. The kind he measured in inches back in Massachusetts, the kind that ruined baseball games and flooded parking lots. But here, in Botswana, *pula* was a sacred noun. It meant rain, yes—but also blessing, wealth, survival, longing. It was the name of the national currency, as if every coin carried a prayer for clouds. It was shouted like an invocation: *"Pula!"*—Hooray! May you eat, may you drink, may your crops not wither. And when it didn't come, people didn't complain. They waited, silently, stubbornly, with patience Chris envied.

It reminded him of something from *Marcus Aurelius*, scratched into the back pages of his journal: *"Receive without pride, let go without attachment."* Pula, the rain, he realized, was exactly that—received without pride, waited for without entitlement. It came when the earth was ready, not when the people were.

As Heaven once whispered under a cloud-choked sky, *"Pula e tla ka masego."* —Rain comes with blessings.

And when it finally fell, on metal roofs, on cattle pens, on scattering chickens—*pula* felt like forgiveness.

She joined him, her presence warm beside him despite the cool mist drifting under the porch roof.

"Do you know what this means?" she asked quietly, eyes on the horizon.

"Hope?" Chris ventured.

"Change," she corrected gently. "Here, rain never just falls—it transforms."

They stood side by side, each lost in thought, both knowing they weren't just speaking about the weather. The village felt different after the weeks of tension, the whispers that had clouded their relationship, and Chris's own illness that had laid him bare.

The storm slowly eased. The air was fresh and crisp, carrying scents of wild sage.

Petrichor rose from the cracked earth like a hymn.

"My mother spoke about you again," Heaven said after a pause, her voice cautious but hopeful.

"What did she say?"

"She said the rain had not washed you away. That perhaps you have roots after all."

Chris smiled softly, feeling oddly grateful. "And you? Do you believe that?"

She hesitated only a moment. "I'm beginning to."

That evening, as they returned home through puddled dirt roads, Chris considered what roots meant in this place.

They weren't just planted—they were chosen.

The earth was stubborn, unyielding.

Yet when it was watered, it bloomed fiercely.

And perhaps, he thought, love was not so different.

September17, 1987

Dear Grandma,

Today it finally rained. Pula! Not gently, not hesitantly, but with a force that felt like the world had let go of something it had clung to far too long. The sky emptied itself without apology, and the dust surrendered, turning to mud. The land bloomed. And I realized, I've been blooming too. Slowly. Awkwardly. But undeniably.

When I came here, I was so certain I was supposed to teach. But I've learned far more than I've taught. I've learned that love doesn't always announce itself loudly; sometimes it grows quietly, stubbornly, even defiantly.

That's how I found myself loving Heaven—not suddenly, but with the steady certainty of water seeping into thirsty ground.

Heaven is everything I didn't know I needed. She's strong yet gentle, wise yet playful. She understands the things I still struggle to name. She teaches me to listen, to be patient, and to embrace discomfort as part of growth.

And this place, Botswana—I arrived with books and plans, believing I could help change things here. I wanted to make a difference. So idealistic I suppose.

I learned to live without certainty, to respect traditions older and wiser than myself, and to find beauty in simplicity—in the shadows cast by firelight, in the laughter shared in a language.

I realize that I'm still learning, though.

I've faced illness, judgment, and misunderstandings. But I've also found acceptance and warmth.

The elders watch me closely, but they've begun to nod instead of whisper. The children tease me openly but smile when I speak Setswana.

And Heaven's mother, who once saw me as a foreigner destined to leave, has begun to see me as someone who might stay.

I'm not sure where life will take us, Grandma, whether we'll remain here or journey elsewhere. But right now, with rain soaking into the earth and Heaven at my side, I can't imagine being anywhere else.

I miss you terribly, yet I carry your wisdom in every step I take.

With the scent of wet earth,
Chris

CHAPTER THIRTY-SEVEN
BETWEEN US, A FLAME

"Not by bloodline, nor by birthright, but by choosing;
we became each other's. — After Ruth

Under the quiet breath of candlelight, Chris felt his insecurities surface again. He watched Heaven quietly stitching a tear in her dress, her expression serene.

"Heaven," he began cautiously, voice taut with apprehension. "Sometimes I worry that I'm not enough for you. That this—us—won't last."

She paused, needle poised midair. Her eyes searched his face thoughtfully.

"Why do you think that?" she asked softly, laying the needle down gently.

"Because I'm always questioning myself. My place here. My right to love you," Chris admitted, eyes lowered. "I keep wondering if you'll eventually realize I'm not what you need."

Heaven moved closer, her hand covering his gently but firmly. "Chris, I chose you. Not lightly, but deliberately. You're more than enough. But I know words alone won't settle your fears."

"But what if—"

She squeezed his hand, stopping him. "Listen. If moving to America proves to you that my love is genuine, then let's go. I would leave everything here behind for you."

The shock of her offer struck like cold water. "No. Heaven, that's not fair to you. I can't ask you to sacrifice your home, your family, your roots."

She smiled, a blend of patience and firmness. "Then trust me when I say my love needs no proof beyond what we've already built. But I want you to feel secure. Your fears matter to me, too."

Chris felt a lump in his throat, emotions rising. "You've given me more reassurance than I ever imagined. So maybe—I should stay. After my Peace Corps commitment ends. Here, with you."

Heaven's eyes softened deeply. "Only if that's truly what your heart desires. Not out of guilt or doubt."

He lifted her hand to his lips, kissed her fingers tenderly. "My heart desires you. And wherever you are, Heaven, that's home enough for me."

In that moment, alongside a single steady flame and whispered promises, the future felt less uncertain. The room was still—the kind of stillness that comes only after truth has been spoken aloud. Not loud truth, but quiet truth shared between two people in the fragile space between doubt and decision. The candle flickered faintly in its clay holder, casting shadows that danced like spirits across the walls, and yet nothing felt haunted.

They had crossed a threshold—not marked by geography, not carved in stone or drawn on a map, but by choice. A decision to be seen, to risk the unknown for the sake of something real.

This was not a leap of emotion alone, but of intention. Of surrender. Like Ruth choosing Naomi's path over her own, saying, *"Where you go, I will go; where you stay, I will stay." (Ruth 1:16).* Not a promise built on certainty, but on conviction. The kind of love that doesn't wait for perfect conditions but instead grows wild in the desert.

Marcus Aurelius once wrote: *"When you arise in the morning, think of what a precious privilege it is to be alive—to breathe, to think, to enjoy, to love."* That privilege isn't just about breath or heartbeat. It's about the courage to stand beside someone not because it's safe, or expected, but because it's human.

They had not solved everything. The world outside continued to spin with its judgments, its borders, its doubts and predispositions. But between that small flame and the faint writing of fire upon the wall, two people had chosen to stand on the same side of a line—not drawn by others, but by their own hands.

True love.

And in doing so, they had not escaped uncertainty.

They had made peace with it.

Together.

October 10, 1987

Dear Grandma,

Tonight, beside the hush of candlelight, I told Heaven I was afraid—afraid that I might not be enough, that love, even the kind that feels like destiny, can buckle under the weight of the world's doubts. She listened the way you used to—with her whole body, like the truth might break if it wasn't handled carefully.

Then she said it: *"Chris, I choose you."*

Not softly.

Not to calm me.

But like a fact chiseled into stone.

And I swear, in that moment, I felt you.

Not as memory.

Not as metaphor.

You.

Like you were there, your hand on my shoulder, your voice folded into hers. I almost turned to answer you. Almost said, *"Did you hear that, Grandma?"*

But then I remembered.

There's no one to send this letter to.

You're gone.

Three years now.

And this—this letter? It has nowhere left to go.

No postman. No mailbox.

Just the space where you used to be.

Through dry seasons and downpours, I've written these letters like they were prayers mailed to heaven without stamps. And somehow, that's where they've always belonged.

Heaven offered to follow me anywhere. Across oceans. Through borders. Into the unknown. But I said no. Not because I doubt her, but because I *trust* her. Because love doesn't need a passport, and home is a person, not a place.

Sometimes when Heaven says my name, I hear it in your voice. And I think: maybe this is how we carry the dead—not in grief, but in grammar. In the way we learn to speak love more fluently.

Marcus Aurelius said: *"Accept whatever comes to you woven in the pattern of your destiny, for what could more aptly fit your needs?"*

And so I've stopped asking if I belong. I simply unfold—like a map with no borders.

The world still insists on neat categories. Who belongs where. Who gets to love whom. But Heaven and I—we've chosen the mess. The mystery. We've chosen each other.

We'll toss a coin—Botswana or America. Fifty-fifty. But really, the outcome doesn't matter. Wherever it lands, we'll land together. Ecclesiastes says: *"Two are better than one, if either one falls, the other can help them up."*

So, I'll keep writing to you. Not because the mail runs that far, but because you still answer.

From wherever you are.

From Heaven.

CHAPTER THIRTY-EIGHT
TWO PULA FOR DESTINY

The air in Chris and Heaven's backyard hung thick with the aroma of braaied boerewors and spiced mopane worms sizzling in a pan, Heaven swearing they added a "mystical zing" to the marinade. Fairy lights, strung loosely between the baobab trees, blinked unevenly, their glow mingling with the chaotic energy of a hundred chattering guests. This wasn't just any party, it was a "Botswana or Bust" send-off, a momentous decision disguised as a feast.

"Honey, are you sure about the blowup zebra?" Chris asked, eyeing the helium-filled behemoth with a mixture of amusement and mild terror. It was currently being wrestled into submission by a group of giggling students. Heaven, resplendent in a dress that shimmered like a thousand sunsets, simply winked. "Think of the photo history, my love! Besides, what's a Botswana party without a slightly deranged inflatable zebra?"

The party was a glorious collision of cultures. Batswana colleagues in vibrant traditional attire mingled with Tlhomo Junior Secondary School students sporting their best attires, while Heaven's eccentric family – a colorful collection from all parts of Botswana – circulated with trays of questionable but undeniably delicious snacks.

Uncle Thuso, convinced he could predict the future through interpreting the flight patterns of dung beetles, was currently engaged in a heated debate with Heaven's mother, MmaHeaven, their Setswana echoing across the yard like rival choirs.

Lesang stood against a morula tree like a prophet out of season, her silence sharp and severe, eyes sweeping the crowd with the calm of a creature that waits until the music quiets and the bones are laid bare.

Naledi lingered in the shadows, eyes glassy, not from a possible goodbye—but from some untouchable future, still waiting to happen.

"The coin, RraGardener! The coin!" shouted RraMmephi, the jovial headmaster. His smile glistened as he held aloft a freshly polished two-pula piece. He displayed it the way a chief might hold a staff at kgotla, half serious, half mischievous. "This is no ordinary coin, my friends. Tonight, it will tell us: Botswana, or America?"

"Right, people, gather 'round!" Chris announced with his voice booming from an oversized megaphone. "Tonight, we decide our fate! Botswana, the land of breathtaking landscapes and surprisingly aggressive spitting cobras, or...the States, the land of...well, you know..."A wave of nervous laughter rippled through the crowd. Heaven's cousin, a self-styled shaman named Mothusi, began a spontaneous drumming circle, the rhythm building to a crescendo of anticipation.

"Remember," Heaven whispered to Chris, her eyes sparkling with a mischievous glint, "no matter what happens, at least we have the inflatable zebra."

The coin, shimmering under the fairy lights, was tossed high into the air, a tiny, shining speck against the vast, star-studded African sky. It spun, it twirled, a symbol of their uncertain future. Heads Botswana, Tails America...and in the final moment before it landed, Chris turned—not toward the coin, but toward Heaven and knew which way his heart had already fallen.

The scene dissolved in a swell of voices—shouts folding into each other like waves, rising into a single, jubilant roar. Whether the coin chose heads or tails was lost in the sound, swallowed by the moment. The helium-inflated zebra, meanwhile, had escaped its captors and was now floating high in the night sky.

EPILOGUE
HORNS OUT, HEARTS OPEN

Most of the guests had gone. Only the faint scent of charred boerewors lingered, clinging to the air like memory. The last of the fairy lights flickered on a low battery, their glow stuttering like a heart unsure whether to stay or let go.

Chris sat with Heaven on the low stone wall behind their house, elbows touching, their silence stitched with the crickets' quiet song.

There was nothing left to say—not yet. The coin had landed. The future had been named. But the naming hadn't made it any easier.

The garden lay in quiet disarray: folded chairs, a tray of untouched beetroot salad, a half-buried sandal no one claimed. The inflatable zebra had floated off sometime after midnight, untethered, swallowed by stars. He wondered if someone in Gaborone would find it in the morning and make a wish.

Moonlight pooled at their feet.

Somewhere nearby, a pair of snails emerged from the damp soil, gliding slow as breath, their tiny tender horns brushing in a moment of communion, a quiet greeting. They paused, hesitating in gentle recognition, then glided onward side by side, yet unbound.

Chris watched them, his throat tightening.

He remembered something from *Meditations*, written by a man who ruled an empire but still feared how easily things slipped away:

"Do not hanker after what you cannot hold.
Everything is borrowed. Even this."

He reached for Heaven's hand.

She took it quietly.

"We'll be alright," he said. Not from certainty, but from the need to speak hope aloud. To give shape to a hope not tied to a destination.

Heaven rested her head on his shoulder.

"We are already roots sharing hidden water," she said. "Even if sometimes we bloom alone."

The snails disappeared into the undergrowth, their silver trails already fading.

The stars above them blinked without urgency. The air was still, expectant.

Whatever came next, they would meet it slowly, deliberately.

Horns out. Hearts open.

THE END

#####

APPENDIX
THE UNITED STATES PEACE CORPS

The United States Peace Corps is one of the most iconic
initiatives in the landscape of American diplomacy and
global service. Since its establishment in 1961, the Peace
Corps has sent hundreds of thousands of volunteers
around the world to serve in countries in need of skilled
support, while promoting mutual understanding between
Americans and host communities. More than just a
development program, the Peace Corps has functioned as
a unique blend of humanitarian aid, cultural diplomacy,
and political soft power.

The Peace Corps was officially created on March
1, 1961, by an executive order signed by President John F.
Kennedy, and later authorized by Congress through the
Peace Corps Act of September 22, 1961. The concept
emerged during a time of intense geopolitical tension—at
the height of the Cold War—and was fueled by Kennedy's
vision of a new generation of Americans committed to
global service.

During a campaign stop at the University of
Michigan in October 1960, Kennedy famously challenged
students to contribute two years of their lives to help

people in developing countries. The enthusiastic response led to the formation of what would become the Peace Corps. From the outset, the program was designed to fulfill three specific goals: (1) to help the people of interested countries in meeting their need for trained men and women; (2) to help promote a better understanding of Americans on the part of the peoples served; and (3) to help promote a better understanding of other peoples on the part of Americans.

At its core, the Peace Corps is about people-to-people diplomacy. Volunteers, usually American citizens over the age of 18, commit to live and work for two years (plus three months of training) in a host country, where they serve in a wide variety of sectors, including education, health, agriculture, youth development, economic development, and environmental conservation.

Volunteers are not military personnel, nor are they part of the diplomatic corps in a traditional sense, but they are nevertheless representatives of the United States. The Peace Corps operates independently, though its director is appointed by the President and confirmed by the Senate, reflecting its status as both a public service and a foreign policy tool.

Since its inception, the Peace Corps has operated in more than 140 countries. However, the specific countries involved change over time, based on need, political relationships, safety, and the host governments' requests. As of recent data, active Peace Corps programs exist in about 60 countries, spanning Africa, Asia, Latin America, the Caribbean, Eastern Europe, and the Pacific Islands.

In the early decades, Peace Corps service was heavily focused on newly independent countries in Africa and Asia, as well as Latin America, where U.S. foreign policy interests converged with local development needs. Over time, regions like Eastern Europe and Central Asia were added following the dissolution of the Soviet Union, as these areas began transitioning to democracy and free markets.

Each Peace Corps program is created in collaboration with host governments and communities. Assignments are demand-driven, meaning that countries request volunteers with specific skill sets rather than having volunteers impose their own agendas.

One of the most remarkable aspects of the Peace Corps is the diversity of its volunteers. While many volunteers are recent college graduates, many others are mid-career professionals or retirees. In recent years, the Peace Corps has actively sought to expand representation across racial, socioeconomic, and age groups.

Though the average age of a Peace Corps volunteer is around 26, the agency has hosted volunteers well into their 70s. Volunteers come from all 50 states and U.S. territories and increasingly reflect the diverse cultural fabric of America itself.

Volunteers often serve in areas vastly different from their own backgrounds, and the immersive nature of their assignments—living with host families, learning local languages, working in underserved communities—leads to profound cross-cultural exchange. Many volunteers describe their experience as transformative, shaping their careers, values, and worldviews.

While the Peace Corps is nominally apolitical, it has long been viewed as an instrument of soft power. Unlike military aid or economic sanctions, the Peace Corps works through personal relationships and grassroots engagement. The underlying premise is that peace is built not only through treaties and statecraft, but also through human connection, shared goals, and mutual respect.

During the Cold War, the Peace Corps functioned as a counterweight to Soviet influence in developing countries. By deploying idealistic young Americans to live among the rural poor and contribute to local development, the U.S. sought to win hearts and minds—and provide an alternative vision to communism.

Even today, Peace Corps service subtly reinforces American values of volunteerism, democracy, and innovation. While volunteers are not allowed to engage in political activities or proselytize, their mere presence as respectful, collaborative guests often challenge stereotypes about Americans abroad.

At home, the Peace Corps has also had a political impact. Many alumni have gone on to distinguished careers in government, education, international development, and public health. Former volunteers include senators, ambassadors, university presidents, and nonprofit leaders.

The Peace Corps has faced criticism over the years, particularly regarding its effectiveness, safety protocols, and adaptability. Some development experts question whether volunteers—many of whom are young and inexperienced—can provide meaningful, sustainable assistance. Others have raised concerns about volunteer safety, especially in regions with political instability or health risks.

There have also been calls to decolonize the Peace Corps, urging it to rethink the power dynamics inherent in sending Americans to "develop" other countries. In response, the organization has made efforts to improve its cultural sensitivity, local accountability, and long-term impact.

The Peace Corps stands as a unique American institution—part idealism, part diplomacy, and wholly human. Its blend of service, education, and cross-cultural engagement reflects the highest aspirations of democratic society. Though imperfect and evolving, the Peace Corps remains a testament to the idea that real change begins not with grand policy pronouncements, but with small acts of courage, humility, and understanding between individuals. As the world faces complex challenges like climate change, global health crises, and economic inequality, the role of initiatives like the Peace Corps is more relevant than ever. It reminds us that peace is not merely the absence of conflict, but the presence of empathy, partnership, and shared purpose.

AFTERWORD
COMMENTARY
by Lesedi Graveline

"I'll slap your black butt right back to Africa." My ears turned red as anger and annoyance erupted from my throat.

"DAD! You cannot say stuff like that" I demanded through clenched teeth. I swear he does that just to get a rise out of me.

He would say, "Oh, stop it. I just say it to see your reaction"

See?

"Mom, how can you just sit there and not do anything but laugh?" I questioned.

"You know nothing about love, Sedi. It's not created. It's recognized," she said in her sweet, gentle accent.

I (respectfully) held my hand up saying, "Yeah, I don't really know what Setswana proverb you translated that from, but I feel like that logic doesn't apply here."

"You see, that's your problem. Love has no 'logic.' You're just like him, I swear. Why can't you just feel your way through things?"

I rolled my eyes. "Okay well I don't really know how I'm supposed to *feel* my way through a boundary HE is crossing. Or should I just *feel* my way through the fact that Black people have been struggling for freedom since the moment they were stolen from the shores of Africa beginning in the 16th century? I could just *feel* the real levity and humor in that sentiment. I could *feel* how the legacy of this wretched past can still be felt throughout the United States today in 2020 and continues to impact the structures that control the fabric of our society. Or I could *feel* how many Americans ignore the truths of the country's violent past and present, a highly problematic response that discounts the harsh realities that Black people, particularly Black women, endure today. I'll just *feel* the truths that include racist characterizations and stereotypes about Black people, which continue to reassert themselves today in increasingly violent ways because of a failure to acknowledge the very history that has fostered them. And then, I'll *feel* how this not only shapes the public perception of Black people, but it also creates the conditions by which a casual disregard for Black lives is acceptable.

They were still nonchalantly making dinner, as if I was missing something that was just too glaringly obvious. I think they stopped listening once I said "shores of Africa." I caught them smiling at each other.

With a furled and confused brow, I continued reading to them the introduction of my most recent graduate school essay.

From Selma to Ferguson and Baltimore: Policing Black bodies and King's Vision for a Better Future

They always had this look like they'd figured everything out. The whole "racism" thing. Well, maybe not all of it. But some things. Like, love. They always made it look so easy. But I wondered what had they endured? What did they know about struggle? Did they know what it was like to be caught between two worlds? Two identities. I was once called "Tituba" as a nickname in my predominantly white high school, then "lekgowa" by my cousin's friends when we would spend summers visiting our family on my mother's side.

My parents met in the Peace Corps in Botswana. My dad volunteered for the Peace Corps and met my mother, born and raised in a village called Serowe, located in Eastern Botswana. She and her best friend were perusing newspaper ads for jobs and came across a call for locals to teach language and culture classes for the Peace Corps. A perfect fit for my mom, who has always had an incredible knack for languages and who is deeply devoted to preserving tradition and educating others. My dad sat in the front row of one of her language classes and they eventually married. They had my older sister, Tumelo (Tumy) then me.

I like to think that Tumy and I had an unusual childhood. Growing up, we spent our summers playing hopscotch and jumping rope with our cousins in the Kalahari Desert. We had both been on several safaris in the African savannah by the time we were 10. My parents made a tremendous effort to make sure that we were traveling to our home country and learning about our family's history and traditions. I think they did this because it was important for them to raise children who would operate on a great deal of integrity; understanding the difference between what's right and what's wrong but also exercising gratitude and appreciation for the education and resources we had access to here in the U.S. They wouldn't allow us to forget where we came from and the responsibility not squander our blessings.

So at a *really* young age, Tumy and I began to understand where we came from and how that was inherently tethered to who we were and who we were going to become. I had an abnormal amount of clarity about the world and my position in it, like the privileges and injustices that came with the family, the country (or village), and skin you were born into. I was truly fortunate for this. However, at the same time, I grew up existing between two vastly different worlds. I was constantly being forced to categorize myself as either Black or white even though in one community I wasn't considered Black enough to be called "African" and in the other, I wasn't light enough to be called "white". Navigating my identity continues to be a never-ending journey for me.

I guess that's what this book is ultimately about. Identity. Race. Boundless love. Navigation in both the literal sense and the metaphorical one. Our unique journeys. And two people who declared their love for one another in a time and place where everything would be uncertain. They were brave and without that courage, my sister and I would not be here.

Setswana Glossary and Pronunciation Guide

Setswana is a tonal Bantu language with vowel-based pronunciation and aspirated consonants. Below is a simplified guide for English readers:

Vowels: a = 'car', e = 'let', i = 'meet', o = 'go', u = 'school'

g: sounds like a deep 'h', as in Scottish 'loch'

kg: aspirated k + h, pronounced separately

kh: strongly aspirated 'k'

ph: strongly aspirated 'p'

tlh: aspirated 'tl', as in 't-lh'

ts: as in 'cats'

tl: as in 'atlas'

ê: as in 'there'

ô: as in 'ought'

Common Phrases

A o na le mathata?— Do you have any problems?

Dumela mma— Hello madam

Dumela rra— Hello sir

Ee, ke na le mathata— Yes, I have problems

Ga a je— He/she does not eat

Ga ke tlhaloganye — I do not understand

Ke a ja— I am eating

Ke batla go ya shopong — I want to go to the shop

Ke lapile — I am tired

Ke tla go bona— See you

Ke tla go bona kamoso — See you tomorrow

Ke tsogile sentle — I woke well / I am fine

Ke tswa Amerika— I am from America

Ke ya lapeng — I am going home

Nnyaa, ga ke rate kofi— No, I do not like coffee

O rata kofi? — Do you like coffee?

O tsogile jang?— How did you wake? / How are you?

O tswa kae?— Where are you from?

O ya kae?— Where are you going?

Re a leboga — We thank you

Tswêê-tswêê— Please

Greetings

Dumela rra— Hello sir

Dumela mma— Hello madam

Dumelang — Hello (to a group)

O tsogile jang?— How are you?

Ke tsogile sentle — I am fine

Re a leboga— Thank you

Sala sentle — Stay well

Tsamaya sentle — Go well

Polite Phrases

Tswêê-tswêê— Please

Intshwarele— Excuse me

Ke a leboga — Thank you

Ke kopa metsi— I would like water

A o bua Setswana? — Do you speak Setswana?

Ga ke bue Setswana— I do not speak Setswana

Conversation

Ke a ja— I am eating

Ga a je— He/she does not eat

O tswa kae?— Where are you from?

Ke tswa Amerika— I am from America

O ya kae?— Where are you going?

Ke ya lapeng — I am going home

Ke batla go ya shopong — I want to go to the shop

Ke tla go bona kamoso — See you tomorrow

Feelings and Needs

Ke lapile— I am tired

Ga ke tlhaloganye— I do not understand

Ee, ke na le mathata— Yes, I have problems

A o na le mathata?— Do you have problems?

Affection

Ke a go rata— I love you

O montle— You are beautiful

Money and Prices

Ke bokae?— How much is it?

Ke bokae gotlhe?— What is the total price?

Money and Prices

General Vocabulary

adima — Borrow

apaya — Cook

araba — Answer

bana — Children

batsadi — Parents

baya — Place; put

bedis — Boil

bereka — Work

bina — Dance

bitsa — Call

bolaya — Kill; injure

boloka — Keep

bolêla — Tell

borotho — Bread

bua — Speak

buka — Book

bula — Open

dijô — Food

dira — Do

dirisa — Use

dumêla — Hello; agree; believe

fa — Give

feta — Pass

fetsa — Finish

fitlha — Bury; hide

fitlhêla — Find

gakolola — Advise; remind

gana — Refuse

go siame — Goodbye

intshwarele — Excuse me

itshwarela — Forgive

itumelela — Be glad

itumêla — Be happy

ja — Eat

kgaitsadi — Sibling (opposite gender)

kgôna — Be able

kopa — Ask (politely)

kopi — Cup

kwala — Write

leka — Try

lela — Cry

lona — You (plural)

lwala — Be sick

malome — Uncle (maternal)

mma — Mother

mmane — Aunt (maternal)

motôgô — Soft porridge

nama — Meat

nna — I; live; sit

ntate — Father

ntlo — House

ntsalake — Cousin

nwa — Drink

phefo — Wind

posa — Post office

rata — Love; like

reetsa — Listen

reka — Buy

rekisa — Sell

robala [— Sleep

rona — We/us

ruta — Teach

sala — Stay behind

senya —Be kind

tla — Come

tlhapa] — Bathe

tlhatswa — Wash

tlisa — Bring

tsamaya — Go

tsaya — Take

tshaba — Be afraid

tsoga — Wake up

tswala — Close

utlwa — Feel; hear; taste

ya — Go

About the Author

M. C. Graveline was born and raised in the quiet hills of central Massachusetts, where curiosity and determination shaped his early years. He studied engineering in college before serving as a commissioned officer in the United States Navy, where he learned the value of discipline, purpose, and perspective. His path then took  an unexpected and life-altering turn when he joined the U.S. Peace Corps and was posted to Botswana as a teacher. There, among hardened red roads, cattle posts, and the warmth of village life, he found a second home—and the inspiration that would one day bloom into a novel. After his return, Graveline built a successful career in the software and aerospace industries, holding several executive leadership roles. Now retired in New England with his wife, he has returned—in spirit and story (and occasionally physically)—to the land that once taught him how to listen, adapt, and truly understand. *This is his first novel.*

PHIKZANA PRESS —LLC—